A.M. HARGROVE

I'LL BE WAITING
A Vault Novella

Copyright © 2018 by A.M. Hargrove

Cover by Dana Leah
Photo by Shutterstock
Editing by Gray Ink

Chapter One

LEE

THE EXPLOSION HIT and the first thing I noticed wasn't the sound. It was the absence of it. The blast exposure had caused a temporary hearing loss, only I wasn't cognizant of that at the time. Disorientation and confusion tossed me into a vortex of the unknown. I blinked once, twice, but nothing cleared my vision. Dizziness prevailed until I was aware that someone was dragging me by the strap of my vest. A face appeared in front of me with lips moving, but confusion reigned. Squinting, I thought maybe I could lip read, but words jammed in my throat like wooden blocks. It wasn't that I couldn't speak—I couldn't breathe. With stark clarity, I knew I was facing my own death.

Dying is a strange thing. Instead of panicking, a sense of calm cocooned me. I was lying on a bed of fluffy down, embraced in the utmost comfort. All the months in the desert sand and heat were wiped away with the snap of my fingers and were replaced by joy and peace. From there I was transported to a crystal clear pool, somewhere near a tumbling waterfall. The aqua water was serenity to my senses as the water was nature's own music. In the blink of an eye, I journeyed to a distant mountaintop with a view unlike any other. I was on top of the world able to see for miles and miles. Until ...

Pain, unbelievable pain, sank its ruthless claws into me and viciously tore me away from my precious view tossing me straight into Hell. Muffled sound coming from a distance assaulted my ears. My vision cleared somewhat affording me a view of the chaos surrounding me. A medic shouted, "She's coming around. I think she's with us." Where had I been? What happened? Focus, I needed to focus. Easy to say, difficult to do with the searing pain coming from my lower extremities. Not to mention, my hearing and sight made me believe I was lying in a cave somewhere.

Lifting my head, I only made it an inch or so before a hand gently pushed it back down.

"Easy there, soldier. You're not going anywhere just yet." Then an oxygen mask was placed over my mouth and I was lifted onto a stretcher. The blue sky above me tilted as my makeshift bed was carried to its next destination. Whatever happened must've been serious enough to warrant a med-evac because I was loaded into a helo. Moments later, the horizon dipped as we headed to a destination unknown and I drifted off.

The blank slate of my mind didn't block out the annoying bleep of the alarm clock that some forgetful person wouldn't shut off. If only I had the strength, I would get off my ass and turn the stupid thing off. Or better yet, pulverize it with a hammer. Who would dare to disturb my perfect sleep? When I found out, I was going to kill the motherfucker.

Bleep … bleep … bleep … bleep.

All right already. Stop that noise! Throwing the blankets off, I went to get out of bed and … what the hell! Where was I? There were people all over the place, lined up in hospital beds. Curtains were half drawn so it was hard to see. But I could hear them moaning. Christ, could I hear the moaning.

"Ah, you're awake," a friendly but unfamiliar voice said.

I shifted to see who it was. A doctor stood next to the bed, smiling. "How do you feel?"

My brows drew together because I wasn't quite sure where to begin.

"I'm sure you have a lot of questions. Do you remember anything at all?"

My head slowly swiveled from side to side.

"I see. Well, I'm Dr. Keith Sanchez. Do you know where you are?

"In bed?" I answered lamely.

"Well, that, but you're at Bagram. You do remember being in Afghanistan, right?"

Bagram Air Base. Afghanistan. Bam! Images dropped into place as the puzzle pieces fit perfectly together in my mind.

"I can see things are coming together for you. Do you remember what happened yesterday?"

Yesterday?

"I … I don't think …" but then it all hit me. The IED. We were patrolling the streets of a village near Kandahar. The intel revealed there may be a terror cell operating nearby and that we should be on high alert. As we were walking I spotted an object, a harmless Coke can laying in the street, next to the curb. Normally, it wouldn't have caught my eye, but it was the way the can was cocked up against the curb with a straw sticking out of the top that grabbed my attention. There was something about it that looked off.

Four of us walked in pairs and we were trained to trust our instincts. That day, I trusted mine. I yelled out as I grabbed my fellow soldier's arm, jerking him behind me with as much force as my body contained. That's when all hell broke loose. Using my body as a shield, I threw myself over him as the fire lit up the street.

"Jared? The others?" I asked.

The doctor smiled. "They're all fine. Only minor lacerations, thanks to you."

"It was the Coke can," I muttered.

"Yes, so they said."

"So how long will I be here?"

"We're making sure you're stabilized and then you'll be transferred to Ramstein."

"Ramstein? Germany?"

"Yes. Your injuries are greater than what we can treat here in the mobile unit."

My voice hitched as I asked, "And what exactly are my … injuries."

His kind brown eyes softened with what, precisely? Pity? Sympathy? This couldn't be good. The V that formed between his brows further confirmed my suspicions.

"Corporal Marston, that IED did a whole lot of damage to you and you're very lucky to be alive. But I'm sorry to inform you that you lost your left leg below the knee. Your right leg is also in pretty bad shape. We need to make some repairs because the bone is damaged, but we don't have the capabilities to do it here. Our imaging isn't state of the art either so it's best if we get you to Ramstein ASAP."

My hand automatically reached for my leg but I could only get as far as my knee. So I tried to sit up, but a surge of dizziness had me doing the fish flop.

"Take it easy. It hasn't been that long since you came out of anesthesia."

"I ... I don't get it. My calf and ankle hurt. How can that be if my leg is gone?" I wasn't prepared to deal with this news.

"Phantom pain. You've heard of it, I'm sure."

"But this is severe."

"Yeah, it can be. No one really knows the cause, but it appears that your brain is getting mixed signals from your body and it manifests itself in the form of pain."

Everything he said made my situation sound more than terrible. Was this my career ender? I was planning on being in the marines for the long term. Now what the hell was I going to do?

Chapter Two

RUSTY

THE SCREAMS WOKE ME UP, but this time they weren't a result of my recurring nightmare. I flew to my feet and jogged to the door.

"What's up?"

My teammate on night duty during this mission answered, "Some disturbance outside. We're checking it out."

"How's the target?"

"We're still waiting to hear," he answered.

"Fuck."

"My words exactly."

"Any news from the command center?" I asked.

"Nothing. If we don't hear anything in the next couple of hours, we're gonna have to move. She won't last much longer and as it is, we have to get through the border with her in this state. It's not gonna be smooth."

"We'll have to storm the building."

"Yeah, that's the plan as of right now. Tonight. We're trying to find a doctor to help us."

I scratched my head. "Our supplies can't do the trick, huh?"

"Not with what we can tell. Her injuries are too severe."

One of the guys returned with a report of what was happening. "They just killed a woman for information on where we're hiding. We can't stay here much longer."

"Okay. Tonight, at dark. We stick to the plan," our commander, Thompson, said.

"What about the doctor?"

"While you were napping, we sent out a couple of guys to work on that. They should be back soon."

And they were, with a physician in tow, who was sympathetic to our cause. He had a vehicle which would transport us to the border. If all this would work, we could make it out safely tonight.

"You do know you could die doing this?" I asked the physician.

"I risk death every day at the hands of the extremists, so what does this matter?"

Thompson walked over to us and said, "You could come with us. Your ticket to freedom."

He shook his head. "I have a family. They would kill them all."

My fellow soldiers and I shared a glance. This was something we were familiar with, as the extremists often did this to the sympathizers.

"They will probably kill you anyway. Once they figure out who aided us in our escape, they'll also kill your family," I said.

"My family is already on their way out of the country, and I will be joining them."

"Where will you go? Let us help you," I insisted.

"Don't worry about me. We will be protected."

It wasn't so much what he said, but the way he said it that made me leery. He wouldn't look me in the eye. We'd been trained to pick on these kinds of nuances. And why was his family already on the move? Was he really going to help us or lead us into another ambush? I pulled my commander aside.

"How much do you trust this guy?"

"Why?"

"Something about what he said makes me itchy. Not only that, the dude is shifty as hell."

"Aw, shit, Garrett. I need more than that." His eyes drilled into mine, so I explained my intuition about his family. It was just too convenient for him to show up like that. After giving it some thought, he radioed Wilson. "Base to R1, how did you vet our healer?"

"R1 to base, local contacts. Over."

"R1, were they trusted, over?"

"Base, in the past, over."

"R1, return to base. Over."

"Copy that, base. Over."

A few minutes later, Wilson showed up. Thompson questioned him, and we then decided our good doctor couldn't be trusted. But at this stage in the game, we had no other choice but to use his skills, not to mention, he provided the wheels. We would change the route, and he would accompany us across the border.

The sun sank, and we waited impatiently. One of us was to remain with the doctor while the rest of the team would surround the building where the two hostages were held. We'd drop the guards, do what we were trained to do, and extract our targets. With precision, we should be out of the country within hours.

"Garrett, you got our link to the other route established?"

"Done," I said.

"You make sure Wilson has a clear path out of here when we leave. He'll be staying behind with Dr. Traitor. The good doctor won't know about the change of plans until we veer off the main road."

"Yes, sir." I went to talk to Wilson. Then we waited. The thing about being on these missions was you had to find the patience to get you through the waiting game. If you allowed it, it would destroy you. And that could ruin the mission.

When our time was up, Thompson made his required speech. "Knights, as members of Gold Squadron, it's my duty to remind you that this is a no-fail mission and as so, it is unrecognized by the US government. Should you be captured, there will be no rescue. This is a full assault mission. Spare no one but your team, the targets, and yourselves."

Then we filed out. The building was only a couple of blocks away. As we left, we were reminded of our radio silence.

We surrounded the building and quietly took out the guards. It was a simple matter really. What wasn't simple was how the damn entrance was wired when we blasted it for entry. We didn't expect it to light up the way it did. It notified the entire fucking city and nearly took us out with it. Taking out the occupants wasn't an issue, nor was grabbing the two hostages, although the woman was in bad shape like we expected. Getting out of town was going to be an issue because every damn human within a mile had heard the explosions go off.

We spared not one second. The wounded woman

would have to wait for any kind of medical attention because our radio silence was broken.

Thompson called to Wilson, "Rovers to base, evac needed now."

"Copy that. ETA in five."

"Rover to base. Make it two."

"Copy that."

We worked with expert efficiency and Thompson radioed our location to Wilson. We heard the shouts coming toward us from a distance.

"I'm not sure if we have time for Wilson to get here."

"Rover to base."

"Base is approaching."

"We're coming toward you. The crowds are restless."

"Copy that."

About then, the van pulled up and we loaded in. Now it was round two. The doctor was in the back to assist the patient. I was in the passenger seat, on the comm link via satellite.

"Rover to command. Set our course," I said.

"Rover you're clear, head straight for four blocks but then you've got issues."

"Command, give us the turn when needed."

"Copy that."

With all the chatter in the car, I was afraid I'd miss something, so I yelled over my shoulder for everyone to stay quiet. About that time, the radio crackled to life again.

"Rover, you're gonna head east at the next street. Follow that until you head out of town."

"Copy that." I checked my map to see where it would take us, and it looked like we'd be headed in the wrong direction.

"Command," I said. "You sure about that?"

"It's the only way. They have every other route

blocked. We're gonna circle around the masses and then get you back on track."

"Copy that." I turned to Wilson. "You heard that. Let's do it."

"Got it."

Somehow, we made it to the border. It took forever and when we got there, our friendly doctor ranted about how he wanted out of the van.

"No can do, buddy," Thompson said. "After we hitch a ride on the winged bird, you can either drive back or walk, but not until then. Unless you want to tell us how you knew about us."

He looked like he was about to shit himself.

"Yeah, we figured your ass out."

His mouth slammed shut and we didn't hear another word out of him. The good thing was, he did our hostage right. Without his help, she may not have made it. He had supplies in the van that we didn't.

A few minutes later, our bird arrived to carry us to Bagram. A medic hopped out, and we carried the wounded asset on board, and then we loaded up. Luckily, the woman was going to make it.

Thompson looked at the doctor and said, "Last chance to come with us."

He shook his head, got out of the back, and walked around to the driver's side. That was the last we saw of him.

"Do you think they'll execute him?" I asked Thompson.

"Don't know. He helped us, but you never know what those people will do."

The bird took off and we safely landed as we all decompressed.

"Man, glad that one's over," Wilson said.

"Hey, good job driving. You must've had a van in your previous life," I said, fist bumping him.

"Yeah. My wife's. I have three kids, dumbass."

"I have van envy now." I waggled my brows.

"You're such a dick." He laughed.

Chapter Three

LEE

THE PLANE RIDE to Germany was shitty. But what could I expect? I was strapped to a bed, my arms loaded with IV's, oxygen running into my nose, and my missing ankle and calf were fucking killing me. What was the point of complaining though? It wasn't like they could give me anything for pain. How did you treat something that didn't actually exist?

"Corporal, is everything okay?"

Now why the fuck would anybody ask me that? What did they expect me to say? Oh yeah, all is fantastic over here. I'm just all fiddle-dee-fucking-doo. I didn't bother to answer. Instead, I gave the guy a thumbs up, saving him from my sarcastic reply. It wasn't his fault I was here. And he was only doing his job. I would seriously have to do my best to hold in my asshole remarks.

Too bad we hit every damn bit of turbulence in the air that night. If someone had asked me if I wanted a hammer to the head, I would've gladly taken it. Put me out of my misery. My hearing had been damaged by the blast. But the noise inside this metal tube was making me batshit psycho. Clanking, beeping, grinding, wheezing, whining, and the list went on and on. I was ready to jump out of my skin.

"Corporal, I'm going to give you a push of something in your IV to relax you."

"That obvious, huh?"

"It's common on these flights," was the response.

"The noise. It's …" I shook my head.

"Yeah. Bad, I know. You get used to it after awhile." The medic smiled at me. At least someone had something to grin about.

A few minutes later, my nerves evened out. Whatever he gave me worked super fast and it was a good thing. Psychotic Lee was gone for now.

"Corporal Marston?"

"Yeah. That's me."

"Feeling any better?"

Nodding, I added, "Call me Lee. I figure if you're nice enough to give me some liquid harmony, we might as well be on a first name basis. What's yours?"

"Jerry. Good to meet you, except I honestly wish it was under better circumstances."

"Makes two of us. But you just did me a solid, Jerry, and I appreciate that."

"Just trying to be good at my job and keeping an eye on my patients is one of them. And talk about a solid—what you did for your guys out there was really something. And sorry, but it's in your record here. I want you to know how proud I am to know you." He actually saluted me even though I'm pretty sure he outranked me.

I tipped my head and half-smiled.

"So, Lee, where's home?"

"Ah, it's a small town in the south. I doubt you've ever heard of it."

"Try me," he prodded.

"You asked. Drummond. You guess the state." Whatever he gave me was making me so sleepy, I could barely keep my eyes open.

"Liquid harmony getting to you, huh?"

"Uh huh. Sorry to conk out on you, man, but I'm gonna take a little snooze." And I didn't wake up until Jerry shook me.

"Hey Lee, we landed and we're going to wheel you off momentarily. I just wanted to give you a heads up."

"What'd you give me? That stuff was a miracle worker."

He grinned and said, "It's my special cocktail for anxious patients." Then he patted my shoulder. "And I want to tell you, even though you don't believe it, things are going to work out just fine for you. Keep your chin up, my friend."

"Will do." But what I really wanted to say was—*I'll believe you when damn pigs can fly*. "Oh, Virginia."

"What?"

"Drummond, Virginia. My home."

"Ha. Gotcha."

Jerry unlocked the mechanisms that held the gurney in place during flight and two servicemen came to wheel me down the ramp in the back of the plane. It was a dismal day here in Germany, not a very welcoming sight. But what did it matter? I would be stuck inside for days, if not weeks. I'd heard about what other people went through after these types of injuries. Months of rehab and the PTSD to deal with. But hey, I was alive, wasn't I? Ooo-fucking-rah for me.

Closing my eyes, I tried to focus on better days. Family always made me smile, especially my little brother and his constant barrage of questions whenever we Skyped. God, I loved that kid. He was going to be crushed by this. I had to stay positive just for him.

My bumpy gurney ride finally ended when I was transferred to a normal sized hospital bed, complete with all the bells and whistles. The first thing I did was raise the head and push down the blankets. I'm not sure what I expected —a furry bunny to hop out with a smile and a bouquet of daisies that included a get-well card? What I got instead was stark reality—a leg minus a foot and ankle that ended at mid-calf. The huge bandage wrapped around my knee and extended to the end of what used to be the rest of my leg. But what shocked me just as much was my right leg. It was wrapped in gauze that was seeped with blood. Not just on the lower part but almost up to my groin. I hadn't thought how severe this could be. Was there a possibility of losing this leg too?

I wanted to run far, far away. But wasn't that the joke? I couldn't even walk. And all of this because of a stupid Coke can. I clasped my hands together to stop them from shaking. Jesus C, I was losing it. Deep breaths, Lee.

One, two, three, four, five, six. Exhale slowly. Repeat.

And then it hit. A full-blown anxiety attack. Jerry's mystery cocktail must've worn off because I was crawling out of my skin, hyperventilating, my face going numb. I couldn't process a solitary thought and the worst part of it all—I was alone. My pharynx was closing off, and the more I tried to suck in air, the tighter it got. My ears were buzzing like a fucking hive of angry hornets as my vision grew spotty.

A nurse walked into my room, and she must've figured out what was happening. Was this an everyday event here?

She ran out and came back with someone else and something was pushed into my IV. It didn't take long for it to calm me down. Maybe Jerry's cocktail? I didn't care by then; I was just happy it worked.

The doctor, or at least that's who I thought it was said, "Keep her on two milligrams of lorazepam." Then he turned to me and said, "Corporal Marston, I'm Dr. Wyatt. Do you mind if I call you Lilou?"

I was still a bit addled and regaining my composure. "Lee. Call me Lee," I said, still breathless. "No one calls me Lilou except my family."

He made a harrumph sound for whatever reason, I don't know. "Lee it is. So, then, we're scheduling you for surgery to get your right leg fixed up then. I'm reviewing everything, and we want to get an MRI and maybe a CT if necessary. We have all the X-rays and tests from Bagram. But our equipment is much better. I also want to look at your left leg just to make sure everything looks good there."

"I thought I didn't have a left leg."

"You have quite a bit of a left leg, Lee. From what I read, you're very lucky. And what you did for your fellow soldiers. You saved your fellow soldiers' lives, you know. No one even saw the IED but you."

"How do you know this?"

"It's right here."

He held up my chart, so it must've been noted there.

"Lee, we get a lot of wounded warriors in here, as I'm sure you can imagine, so when someone like yourself comes in, we find out everything we can about him or her. We owe it to soldiers such as you. You're out there risking your lives for your fellow man and you proved that by what you did. That takes more than courage. It takes a heart of gold and the soul of a warrior. That's what you are, Lee.

Now rest easy. We're going to do our very best to get you out of here and on your way stateside to recuperate. But we want to get you back there in the best shape we can. We're going to do you right. You understand me?"

"Yes, sir."

He gently squeezed my shoulder and walked out of the room. The nurse told me to press the button any time if I needed anything.

The next week was muddled in my head. It was filled with scans and surgery. Not one, but three. One on the left leg to complete what had been started in the mobile hospital and two on the right. After four weeks at Ramstein, I was transferred to Walter Reed National Military Medical Center in Bethesda, Maryland.

My parents met me there. Mom cried and cried and Dad did too. I was too numb to do anything. They stayed for a week and returned to Drummond while I endured yet another surgery on my right leg. The IED had done extensive damage to my femur and quad so a lot of repair was necessary, but I got to keep my right leg. After the final surgery, I had to go through rehab and learn to walk again. Both legs had atrophied from being in bed for all those weeks, so I had a tough road ahead and wasn't looking forward to it.

Chapter Four

RUSTY

"YOU OPEN YOUR MOUTH, kid, and I'll beat your ass till you can't ever walk again. You hear me?"

"Yes, sir." I hated him. I hated him more than anything. I wanted to ball my hand into a fist and knock every tooth in his head out. But I didn't stand a chance. I was nothing but a scrawny kid.

Velvet came out of her room, all scrunched up like. She wore that thin looking sweater, the one with the buttons on it. She wore it a lot, even when it was scorching hot outside. I knew why. It was so the kids at school didn't see all the bruises on her arms. I heard what he did to her every night. I could hear her screams. Mom heard it too. It's why she was drunk all the time. I couldn't stand to hug her anymore. Even in the mornings, she smelled like beer or whiskey.

"Get a move on. The train's leavin'." Dad walked out the door and we followed like robots. If we didn't, he'd beat us before we got in the car. One morning, I left my school binder on my bed. I made the mistake of telling him. He popped me right on the cheek. I lied to my

teacher and said I fell down. If I told the truth, Dad would kill me for real.

It was Velvet's sixteenth birthday today. I made a card for her and stuck it in her backpack when she was in the bathroom. I wished there was some pretty present I could buy her, but I didn't have any money to spend. After school, we waited for Mom to pick us up.

"I'm sorry about my dad."

"Not your fault, Rusty."

"Just the same, I'm sorry. Wish there was something I could do."

She gave me the saddest smile I'd ever seen. "I wish my mom was still alive."

"Me too."

Mom pulled up and we got in the car. She stunk something awful. She shouldn't be driving so I watched the road real close to be safe. Only I wasn't so sure what I'd do from the passenger's side. We made it home safe and sound.

That night, I was in my room, lying in bed, and I heard Dad go into Velvet's room. I was thinking he was going to beat her like usual. Only this time something different happened. He did something worse, something uglier. I wanted to help. I wanted it to stop. For the first time since I was a little kid, I cried. Holding my hands over my ears, I lay in the bed and prayed. I asked God to kill my dad for me. I wanted him to die for what he was doing to Velvet.

The next morning, I saw him. He knew I knew what happened. He pulled me outside by my shirt collar.

"You'd better keep your mouth shut if you know what's good for you." Then he pushed me down on the ground and kicked my leg so hard, it took two weeks before I could walk without it hurting.

Was it a sin to want someone to die, because I prayed for his death every single night of my life?

Chapter Five

LEE

TWO MEN HELD me up with the belt around my waist and ropes that were attached to rings on it. I held onto parallel bars to support myself. My leg that had been amputated was propped up on a knee walker and the other one was shaking as I supported myself on it.

"Shit! I can't believe I used to run half marathons. This is ridiculous."

"You've been in bed for weeks, Lee. What do you expect?" It was JB that spoke.

"Yeah. You're not Supergirl," Danny said.

"Shut up. Just don't say anything else. Neither of you needs to remind me of where I've been. Ugh." One more step and I was groaning. "Fuck me. This is brutal."

"You sure cuss a lot for a girl," JB chastised me.

"You sound like my mother," I retorted.

"Well, you do. Wait. I take that back. You cuss a lot, period."

"If I didn't need to hang onto to these damn bars for dear life, I would so flip you off."

Danny moved in front of me, saying, "Yeah, yeah, yeah. Idle threats. Take it like a woman why don't you?"

"One of these days, I'm going to kick that skinny ass of yours, you little shit." And right now, I wasn't even close to joking.

JB looked at me and then at Danny. "Dude, I don't think she's kidding. I'd back down if I were you."

"Seriously?" Danny asked JB.

"As a heart attack, dude. Look at her. Smoke is about to shoot out of her nostrils."

"Good thing she can't catch me then, huh?"

"Why you little sonofabitch. One day I'm going to clean your clock and shove my foot up your ass so far ..."

"Hey, hey, hey, calm it down Mike Tyson." JB was waving the peace sign at me. But I was so pissed I took about five steps right toward Danny.

"And would you look at that." Danny had a smug look on his face. "I knew I could get her pissed off enough to forget about everything and do the dirty."

"The dirty?" I asked.

"Yeah. Walk. You've been saying how hard it was. And how weak you were. I only took your mind off it and put it somewhere else. Now go get 'em, tiger."

He walked behind me and then gave my ass a good hard slap.

"You're trying your damnedest to piss me off, aren't you?"

"Damn straight I am. You're so hard headed it's the best way to get you going. Now move it, grunt." Danny laughed.

"Hey, that was really low. I might be a jarhead with half a leg, but I'm no grunt."

Danny couldn't let it go. "No, but your head is as soft as a grunt."

JB, who had been silently watching our exchange up to this point finally said, "Are you two sure you're not brother and sister?"

"Ew," I groaned. "That's just gross."

"My own sentiments." Danny looked equally as repulsed.

"Wait a damn minute. What's wrong with being my brother?" I asked.

"Because you sound like you've been laying in the gutter for years, trash mouth. No sister of mine would ever talk like that."

My mouth clamped shut so hard my teeth rattled. What the fuck? Was I that bad? Did I need to rein it in?

I was considering my vermin vocabulary when JB said, "You are golden. Congrats, girl. You have reached a new level!" I looked down to see that I had made it to the end.

"I've never done this before." Both guys put their fists out and I bumped them. "Do you really think I'm a trash mouth?"

They both stared without answering.

"Oh, come on guys."

JB's brows lifted and Danny shrugged. But that was it. JB grabbed my wheelchair while Danny unbuckled the belt.

"Princess, your carriage has arrived. Don't forget to do your leg lifts, your majesty, and we shall see you tomorrow. Your ride back to the palace awaits."

I stuck my tongue out at them as I sat on my wheels and headed home for the day. Trash mouth. Maybe I needed to clean up my act. Or at least tone it down. I hadn't used a filter much ever since the accident. Accident, my ass. The fucking bomb that those ratfaced bastards had intentionally left for us to stumble upon. Lucky for us I spotted the thing. Or we all would have been strumming harps right now. Well, maybe some of us. I probably would've been stoking the fires with coal.

"Marston, you up for some chess?"

Looking across the room, I noticed a fellow amputee who I regularly matched up with begging for a game.

"Nah, not right now. I'm tired from PT. Maybe later."

"Pussy."

I flipped him off and kept on rolling. The truth was, I wasn't in the mood for company. Even though I spent more time with JB and Danny than anyone else here, they had gotten the best out of me, and now I wanted the rest of the day to myself. Only problem was, every time I closed my door, I heard the blast. And then the screaming. The question I had no answer for was—who was screaming? A voice in the back of my head always answered me. *It's you, dumbass.* I was the one screaming in pain. Yelling out in agony. Then I would sit alone in my room for hours and shake.

My parents came out to visit as often as they could, but I was about four hours away from them and they both worked. I put on my happy face when they were here, but even though I hated to say it, I was glad to see them leave each visit.

One day after a particularly nasty session with my resident torturers, JB and Danny, there was a knock on my door and I told whoever dared to disturb my quiet time that they better have a damn good reason for doing so.

The door swung open and in strode a woman who was probably the tallest one I'd ever seen. Not that I was one to notice these things—okay I was a liar. I did notice. How could I not? She had legs that almost reached the ceiling. And long dark hair that nearly hit her ass. She stood in front of me and eyed me for a long, painful minute. I started squirming.

"You about ready?"

"Ready for what?" I asked.

"To talk. You've been here going on four months now and all you do is mope around. That's over. Starting right about"—she checked out her watch and said—"now."

"Who are you?"

"I'm the bitch who's going to kick your ass from hell and back, that's who."

And damn if she wasn't kidding. No one told me about Marianna Perez. Or I should say, Dr. Marianna Perez, resident psychiatrist, specializing in PTSD. In other words, take no shit off of anyone for any reason whatsoever, Dr. Perez. And I tried. Man did I try. I handed more crap to her on a silver platter, but she threw it right back in my face. At one point, she actually accused me of faking! Told me I wouldn't know PTSD if it busted down my door. She finally tore me down and built me back up, piece by piece, into the person I used to be. No, I take that back. She made me into something I had only dreamed of being before. Or at least got me pointed in the right direction. I knew I had lots of work to do. I was bitter about losing my leg, more bitter than I could come close to admitting. But that was okay. It was how I dealt with the bitterness that counted. And she helped me figure all that out.

I was inching closer to going home—my real home in Drummond. Therapy was getting better and better. My new prosthesis was on order and when that came in, I would learn how to walk in it. After that, I would be permanently discharged from the marines. I sat in the rec room, laughing at something one of the other guys said when I happened to glance up and saw Jared—Jared, the guy I pushed out of the way of the IED.

He was in full uniform and looked amazing. Behind him stood Randy, Will, and Mark—all of the guys that were with me that ugly day. It was an awkward moment for about two seconds until I waved at them and grinned.

"What are your sorry asses doing here?" I needed something to break the ice, so I thought I'd go with what I used to say to them. It worked.

They all charged over and dropped down so they could hug me. Three tough guys that could barely speak because I suspected their emotions had their tongues all knotted up.

Finally, Jared said, "I owe you my life and my family sent you this." It was a picture of his family—he, his wife, and kids holding up a sign that said *Thanks for saving our dad, Lee.* Now it was my turn to shove back the traitorous tears that collected in the corners of my eyes.

Mark and Will gave me cards from their wives that were very emotional as well.

Mark said, "My wife, Jill, wanted to come, but I wouldn't let her."

"Why not?"

"I wanted this to be just the guys."

"Excuse me. Last time I checked, I still had my female bits."

"Yeah, but you know what I mean. We needed to share this time. And then next time we'll get together with the spouses."

"Okay. We'd better," I said.

Will jumped into the conversation. "Oh, if we don't, Trisha will kill me, so this is already a done deal. She wants to personally hug your neck."

I lowered my head to wipe my tears. I couldn't let them see me cry.

"It's okay, Lou. We've all cried like fucking babies," Jared said.

"Thank God." I held out my arms and we all hugged again. Then we sat around talking for awhile and they wanted to know if I could go out to eat with them. I had honestly not been out of the hospital for so many months that it freaked the hell out of me, so I politely declined. But I promised that when I was finally sprung out of the joint, we would make it a point to have another reunion.

After they left, I realized Dr. Perez was right. Even though my actions cost me my leg, they had also saved four lives, including my own. I thought about Mark, Will, and Jared, and then their families. I wasn't ashamed of the tears that spilled down my cheeks. Yes, I was minus part of my leg, and yes, I was fighting to get my life back. But what would their families have been experiencing if I hadn't seen that Coke can? How would they have gone on without their husbands and fathers? It was a small price in comparison when you put it into perspective.

A couple of weeks later, I mastered my prosthesis—which was a lot harder than I ever thought it would be—and was cleared to go home. With my honorable discharge in hand, I was soon off to the airport, my final destination: Drummond, Virginia.

Chapter Six

LEE

FOLLOWING THE SEMI-ROUGH LANDING, the flight attendant asked everyone to remain in their seats until I deplaned first. I wasn't one who liked attention, so it was more than slightly embarrassing for me. Nodding my thanks, I grabbed my cane and walked off the plane. Drummond didn't have an airport, so I landed in the closest town to it. It wasn't a very large airport, but it did have a jetway that attached to the plane which I was thankful for since it was raining. The crummy weather seemed to follow me around every time I flew. Mother Nature had a shitty sense of humor sometimes.

When I got to baggage claim, Mom was there with my little brother Glenn, waiting. Scuttlebutt—my nickname for him—came barreling up to me and nearly knocked me over.

"Show me your fake leg," he hollered.

"Christ, hold your voice down, you little shit," I said in his ear. Cartoon-like eyes caught mine for a second, then he doubled over laughing.

"I'm telling Mom," he said, acting the tattletale.

"If you do, I'll stick this cane up your ass."

Then he let out the loudest snort this side of the Mississippi. We hugged and both died laughing.

"What are you two up to over there?" Mom asked as she caught up with us.

"Oh, nothing," Scuttlebutt said.

"I told him he was going to be my pack mule for almost knocking me down," I answered.

"Glenn, be easy on Lilou. Her balance might be a bit off."

"No kidding. Call me half-leg."

"Lilou!" Mom admonished me. Glenn snorted.

"No use beating around the bush, Mom."

"Are you gonna get one of those cool legs runners have with those springs?" Scuttlebutt asked.

"Maybe. If I get off my ass and run some." He snickered as Mom sucked in her breath. "It's okay, Mom. My psychiatrist told me not to hold in my feelings when dealing with PTSD." I turned to Scuttlebutt and winked. I doubt Mom bought it, but whatever.

The buzzer went off indicating that luggage was about to drop. "Dude, you sure your muscles can handle my stuff?"

My brother held up his arm and flexed. I wanted to laugh because the scrawny teenager looked like he had an egg sitting on top of the skinny end of a baseball bat.

"I got it Lilou. You can count on me."

"Yeah, I can see that."

He jogged over to the conveyer belt and waited for my

ginormous duffle. It was one of the first ones to drop, followed by my backpack. I didn't carry anything on board with me on account of that dang cane. Mom grabbed my backpack while Scuttlebutt grabbed the duffle. Or tried to. When he went to hoist it off the belt, his face turned the color of an eggplant.

"Dude, you better start lifting some weights," I teased. A man standing next to him gave him a hand and he thanked him.

"How we gonna get this to the car?" baby bro asked.

"A skycap. Watch this." I raised my arm up in the air and yelled, "Can I get some help here, please?"

A man with a cart showed up a minute later and off we went.

Taking in the sights as we drove home from the airport, I tried to remember when I was home last. As if she read my mind, Mom said, "Three Christmases ago."

"I'm sorry it's been so long."

"Why? It's not like you haven't been busy or ..." her voice trailed off. Last Christmas I was in Walter Reed and not fit for human company.

"Yeah, I remember."

Silence settled into the car like a giant cloud, snuffing out the light banter that had been taking place. Even Scuttlebutt grew strangely quiet. I knew I should say something to lift the heavy atmosphere, but I found myself caught up in the scenery as the car sped by. It had been so long since I had been home; I was noticing how much things had changed.

We turned the corner that headed down Main Street, and up ahead sat the old train depot, the one that stood empty for all those years. The town had debated whether or not to tear it down, turn it into a museum, use it for public events, but it seemed no one could ever come to an agreement on anything. As we neared the old building, I was aware that the interior lights were on and for some odd reason, I felt this indescribable urge to go inside.

"Stop the car!" I yelled.

Chapter Seven

RUSTY

THE TEAM HAD LANDED BACK in Virginia Beach at the Naval Air Station. The debriefing took much longer than usual because what was supposed to have been an in and out simple extraction turned out to be anything but. We were part of The United States Naval Special Warfare Development Group or what we referred to as DEVGRU. Most civilians knew us as Seal Team Six, only that wasn't exactly correct. Seal Team Six had been disbanded in 1987 when Seal Team 8 and DEVGRU were formed. However, the moniker stuck, especially with the media. So most people still went with it.

Our mission had been to drop into Iran, rescue two hostages, and then get to the border of Afghanistan for an airlift. Only it didn't quite happen as scheduled. The first problem came when one of the hostages ended up being critically wounded, which we hadn't been aware of. Then our extraction vehicle didn't show. From there, things deteriorated. We couldn't get air support without Iran's knowledge, so we were on our own for twelve hours. What had looked like a piece of cake was a FUBAR like I hadn't seen in over two years.

We finally were able to get the wounded stabilized with the assistance of Dr. Traitor and then made our escape to the border using the vehicle he so kindly lent us. It was touch and go all the way. A bird finally showed up to take us to the base at Bagram. We made it by the slices of our asses.

The explanations to the superiors went on forever. They couldn't understand why it went south so fast. And honestly, neither could we. It was like someone was expecting our show up. And Dr. Traitor's help only added to that explanation. It was too late for guessing games now. We were done and gone. Each of our written reports were expected by tomorrow. I couldn't wait for the couple of weeks leave I had coming up.

My foster sister, Velvet, had been begging me to visit her in California. She was a famous actor now, and had changed her name to Midnight Drake, and her husband, Harrison, owned a PR company that specialized in shining up tarnished images in the entertainment industry. That's how they met, in fact. They were both so busy, though, and they'd recently had a second child, that going out there wouldn't exactly be the needed R&R that my mind and body craved. I would make it a point to head out there in the near future, but right now, I'd stick around here. Maybe head to the beach for a few days or go inland to fish the rivers. I wasn't sure, maybe do some exploring of the local towns around here that I'd always had wanted to do but never got around to.

"Hey, Garrett? You up for a beer?" Greg, one of my teammates asked.

"Sure, man. But I want to get that report written first, so I'll meet you out."

"Sounds good. See you later."

I grabbed my gear, closed my fenced-in locker, and headed to my truck. The drive home didn't take too long. Traffic out this way wasn't bad, and I was determined to finish my work.

Happy I'd gone through the drive-thru of a local eatery on the way home, I pulled out the food and chowed down. I was starved, having not eaten since before lunch. Then I opened my secure laptop and went to work. These briefs were so damn tedious, I was careful to include every detail. It took me longer than I expected, but I didn't hit send. I wouldn't do that until I read it with fresh eyes in the morning.

Then I left for the local hangout to meet the guys. When I got there, it was obvious they'd all had a few. Maybe more than a few.

"So, Garrett, don't you have leave coming up?"

"Yeah, next week."

"Whatcha got planned?"

"Nothing so far."

"You gotta get out of here," Wilson said.

"Oh, I plan to. I just don't know where yet. Maybe I'll go fishing."

"Too bad duck season isn't here yet. My wife's uncle has a place not too far from here." Wilson held his arm out like a shotgun and took aim.

"Hey, I'm up for that anytime, man."

We drank a couple more—well they did—and I gave them all rides home. I was wiped.

After I brushed my teeth, I flopped on the bed. The last thing I remembered was thinking *heaven*. My lids slammed shut the minute I hit the pillow. Sleeping on those military planes sucked.

My internal alarm clock woke me at six a.m. For once I wished I could sleep longer. But that would never happen. My need for food and coffee didn't allow it. The refrigerator was empty, so I hit the shower and headed to the local cafe. They pretty much knew me here and greeted me with a cheery *Good morning*.

I took my usual seat at the counter and my coffee cup was filled immediately while the waitress asked if I wanted my usual.

"You know it, ma'am."

"I've missed you. You've been away."

Laughing, I said, "Are you always this observant?" It wasn't that difficult since I ate here pretty much every morning.

"No, I just notice when my Seals are absent. Been on a mission?"

"Yes, ma'am."

"Hope it went well."

I dipped my head. She knew I couldn't say anything and she never pressed. Her name was Dottie and she was probably my mom's age … if my mom hadn't drunk herself into an early grave.

A few minutes later, a piping hot plate full of scrambled eggs, bacon, hash browns, and two biscuits appeared in front of me. "Here you go, son."

"Ah, thanks. This looks great." Then she refilled my empty cup.

"Anything else?"

"No, this is perfect."

She smiled and left me to eat. I polished my plate and left her a large tip, exactly like I always did. As I was walking out, she hollered out her thanks.

When I got back home, I double-checked my brief to

make sure it was clear, concise, accurate, and error free. When I was satisfied with it, I hit send. Then I set off to the base. The rest of the week went easy. Nothing unusual popped up, which was nice. I didn't want anything to get in the way of my leave.

On Friday, I double checked to see if my leave was still approved. Still not sure of what I would do, I went home to make some plans.

I googled things to do in the area and landed on a couple of small towns, but one called Drummond seemed intriguing. It was an old railroad hub that had apparently been developed into an artsy place with some bed and breakfasts, local shops, and a museum chronicling the railroad when it was a major mode of transportation. The town fascinated me with its antique stores, locally made furniture, and shops that catered to local businesses. It was less than an hour from here so if it turned out to be a bust, I could always head back home.

I made a reservation at a cool looking inn for the following week and decided to check it out. Who knows what I'd turn up?

Chapter Eight

LEE

TO SAY I scared my mother to death would be appropriate. She hit the brakes and I almost went through the windshield, or at least that's what it seemed at the time.

"Mom!"

"What? You told me to stop."

"Not like that. Jeez."

"Well, I'm stopped now. What did you want, Lilou?"

"I saw lights on in the old depot."

The look Mom gave me was one for the record books. "For Pete's sake Lilou. It's a cafe now. It opened about six months ago. Food's real good too. And they opened a museum right behind it. The town's taken an upswing. You'll be pleasantly surprised."

I stared at the red brick building and thought how cool it was that they hadn't torn the place down. "Hey Mom, is this the same train depot that your grandfather came home to when he got back from the war?"

Mom smiled. "It sure is. Grandma used to tell the story all the time. How sad she was that he came home and there was no one to meet him at the train. You know, Lilou, you two probably had a lot more in common than you know."

"How's that?"

"When he was in France, he lost his leg when a grenade exploded."

Wow. I didn't know that part of his story.

That night, I pulled out old picture albums of my great-grandfather. Then I asked my mom everything I could think of.

He served in the military and lost his leg when grenades were thrown into a barn his troop had been hiding out in. When he finally made it back to Drummond, no one had been at the train depot to meet him. Sadly, while he'd been away, he'd received a *Dear John* letter. That's when he decided to go to that same train station every day to meet and greet the soldiers as they returned because he didn't want anyone else to experience what he did. It was how he'd met my grandmother. She'd heard about him and went there one day to see him. They fell in love and ended up getting married.

The following morning, after I did my physical therapy exercises, I dressed and got in my car. It had been so long since I had driven, it felt strange. As I thought about it, it was a good thing my left leg had taken the hit. Otherwise, I would've had to learn how to drive with my prosthesis. My physical therapist said it was time to ditch the cane. My strength in both legs was great and I had demonstrated excellent mobility. He asked about my comfort level and confidence in moving around without it. I walked around the facility for about a half hour and it actually felt better than with it. He said it had to do with the fact that now when people saw me, they didn't see anything that indicated I had any injuries.

"What about my limp?" I asked.

"What limp? I don't see any limp."

I watched myself in the mirrors that ran the length of the room and I could see it—but barely.

"Only you can tell if it's there, and it's so slight you have to stare to notice it."

That was the last time I used the cane.

On the way home, I stopped by the cafe. The urge to revisit the train depot had kept me up most of the night, so it was almost comforting to walk in and take a seat at a small table next to the window. I could imagine my great-granddad sitting here as a voice interrupted my ruminations.

"Can I get you something to drink?" A menu appeared in front of me and I glanced up. Long sandy hair arranged in an array of waves that crowned a face with a familiar grin greeted me.

"Jackson? Jackson Blackburn?"

"Lee? Lilou Marston! Oh my God! What a surprise. I thought you were in North Carolina. Or something like that."

"Yeah, well, that was a while ago. I'm home for good now. And you? You're working here? I was so excited to see this place was a cafe."

"Really? Well, I was the fool who decided to give it a go," she laughed.

"Wait. You're the owner?"

She shrugged a shoulder. "Yeah. It's always been a dream of mine."

"You never said anything about that before. You know, back when we were wreaking havoc in high school." I grinned at her.

"Those were the good old days, yeah?" she asked with a twinkle in her eye.

"Ha! We were always off to no good. Remember that time we stole your grandma's moonshine?"

"Oh, God. But we didn't know it was white lightning until we could barely walk. And talk about sick. Ugh!"

Then we both covered our mouths and burst out laughing. "The school called our parents and they had to come and pick us up. Oh boy, did I get in trouble."

"So did I. And from Granny for stealing that stuff!"

"So, a cafe, huh? How did I not know you had these ambitions?"

She scratched her cheek for a second before saying, "That's because I never told anyone. I thought I'd be the laughingstock of the class. You know, Jackson the burger flipper or something. But I'm actually professionally trained in the culinary arts and I love what I do."

"That's great to hear. And I'm so happy to see you did it in this building. I've always loved this old train depot."

"I just hope the business holds out. It's been up and down. The town is growing and things are picking up, but it takes a lot to run this place, so we'll see."

"My fingers are crossed for you."

"Thanks."

"I hate that we lost touch over the years, but being deployed overseas sort of ..." I swallowed. The words got stuck.

"Hey, I can't begin to understand. But Lee, don't even say another word. I'm just glad you came in."

"Yeah, me too."

I scanned the place, checking it out. It wasn't like I was an expert or anything, but maybe I could help in some way. Only I spotted an adorable train depot set up as a classy cafe, with round bistro tables, crisp linen tablecloths, and artwork that dotted the walls reminiscent of a time long past. I immediately thought of my great-grandfather again.

Jackson's voice cut through my daydreams. "I'll be right back with your …"

"Coffee, please." If she wasn't getting business, it couldn't be the ambiance. This place was charming. Maybe her cooking sucked. I would know soon enough. Checking the menu, I decided on an omelet and some pancakes. When she came back with my java, I placed my order, and off she went.

From the looks of things, she was a one-man show. I hated that for her. Even though we hadn't seen each other since high school graduation, it was because we went our separate ways—I joined the marines and she went on to school. She had huge ambitions. I couldn't afford college, so I did what I thought would get me ahead.

My family wasn't poor by any means. But both my parents had to work to pay the bills. They didn't have the extra money to send me to college, so I decided I would join the military. It was purely a financial decision so I could attend college one day. But once I left Drummond behind, I grew to like the marines. It was regimented and structured, a lifestyle I thrived in. I wasn't one who counted the months, weeks, and days until I was discharged. In fact, I wanted to make a career out of it until … that fateful day. But now I was going to concentrate on getting my degree at the community college and perhaps even going on to law school eventually.

Seeing Jackson reminded me of our youth together, when we were silly and foolish. It's surprising the way we both behaved we ended up doing anything constructive with our lives.

"What's got you grinning like that?" she asked as she set two plates heaping with food in front of me.

"Jeez. That looks yummy." And it did.

"I hope you're hungry." Right then, my belly let out the loudest gurgle.

"Oops." We laughed. "Can you sit?"

She took a quick glance to make sure the other patrons were taken care of. "Only for a second. Everyone's covered for now."

I stuffed the forkful of food into my mouth and my eyes bulged. "Mmm. This is so good," I managed to say around my mouthful of omelet.

A grin stretched across her face. "Yeah?"

"Mmmhmm." Next, I cut a triangle into my pancakes and took a bite. They melted on my tongue. "Holy shit, Jackster. What's in these?"

She cracked up. "My secret recipe."

I swallowed and quickly cut out another triangle as I said, "Oh, come on. It's not like I'm ever gonna make them. I hate to cook." And I plunged the yummy triangles into my mouth. She eyed me as the breakfast vanished. My man-sized appetite took over.

"Christ, woman, how in the world did you eat all of that? Do you have a hollow leg or something? That was a lot of food and you inhaled every morsel of it."

"Yeah." My voice was dead serious.

"Yeah what?"

"I do have a hollow leg."

She laughed, but then stopped when she noticed I wasn't joining in. "What do you mean?"

"Actually, it's not really hollow all the time. Only when I take it off."

Her brows crunched up to form a V in the center. "What the hell are you talking about?"

I lifted my leg and moved it from its place beneath the table. Stretching it out, I knocked on it with my knuckles.

"This. It's fake. When I take it off, it's hollow. Made out of some kind of acrylic."

Her hazel eyes went from curious to soft in a flash. "Oh, Lilou. What ... what happened?"

"You can ask me whatever. It was an IED. A Coke can of all things. I saw it against the curb and ..." I shrugged, then told her the rest of the story. It was pretty surreal telling my old friend how I lost my leg. She was the first *outsider* I had the pleasure of watching hear the story. It wasn't a good thing either.

"Lee, I'm so ..."

"Jackson, please don't tell me you're sorry. You didn't do anything, so there's no need."

She squinted at me, assessing. "Were you alone?"

"No. Three others were there."

"Did they survive?"

I touch her arm. "They're all fine." It's the first time I say it with pride—not because of what I did, but because they didn't die that day.

"Any injuries?"

Shaking my head, I said, "Only minor ones."

She let out a long sigh. "I can't imagine going through what you did. You're so brave, Lee."

A change of topics was in order. Scooting my chair closer, I asked, "Have you done any advertising?"

She leaned forward, resting her elbows on the table. "No, it's not in my budget."

"I'm no expert by any means, but maybe you ought to try a little. And what about social media?"

She chuckled. "Yeah, that's not up my alley, ya know?"

"Why don't I help you some?" And then I thought maybe she's married and her husband wouldn't like it if he knew I was up in her business. "That is if you won't get in trouble or anything."

She cocked her head, reminding me of a puppy trying to identify a noise. "Why would I get into trouble?"

My face began to heat and without a doubt, my cheeks must've been spotted with pink. "You know. With your husband or something."

"Oh." Her hand slashed through the air. "That didn't last. When he realized it took a lot of hard work and late nights to become a famous chef, he dumped me like a hot iron skillet."

My chin must've hit the table because a long finger reached out and pushed it up to close my mouth. I hadn't known she'd gotten married. I was only taking a wild guess, but married and divorced. Whoa.

"Wow. I'm so sorry. I didn't know."

Her narrow shoulders sagged a bit, but then lifted and straightened. "I took a chance on love and it kicked me in the ass. What can I say?"

Now didn't that make me feel even guiltier? My hand covered my heart because I could've sworn it pinched my insides. Who would do that to someone?

"Lee, do you really think you can help me?"

"I just might. We can set up a Facebook page for the cafe and start boosting some posts to grab attention. Maybe hand out some flyers or hang some in nearby towns and such, and do some posting on Instagram. Easy stuff that's either free or super cheap. And maybe we can get a few restaurant critics over here to try out the food. Breakfast and lunch, right?"

"Ideally, I'd like to be open for lunch and dinner, but right now I'm focusing on breakfast and lunch until the word gets out. I can't afford much help, so I can run the breakfast crowd."

Before I gave it any thought, I blurted out, "I can help in here. I don't know a whole lot about working in a restaurant, but you can train me. And I'm free. I don't need the money and until classes start in the fall, I'm available. Deal?"

She squinted at me long and hard. "I feel like I'm taking advantage of you."

"No. I want this cafe to make it. This depot has been around a long time. It has meaning to this town. We only need to make the people believe in it."

She held out her hand and said, "Deal. To old friendships."

"To old friendships."

When I put my palm against hers, I knew this was going to be much more than a summer job. A vision of my great grandfather passed before me in a flash. My great grandmother was walking toward him, wearing a lovely yellow dress and matching hat, and he was grinning like he'd just won the lottery. In the background, I could see the train depot. Deep in my heart, my great grandfather was letting me know this was an omen of great things to come.

Chapter Nine

RUSTY

THE TOWN of Drummond wasn't exactly the bustling hive like the internet had led me to believe, but it was definitely homey. And cute. Yeah, cute. That was a good word for it. Not the place a man like myself wanted to spend a whole lot of time. If word ever got out to the rest of the team that this was where I'd come for part of my leave, I'd never hear the end of it.

Since I was here, I might as well check out the town. Main Street was lined with shops catering to tourists, as the internet said, but most were geared toward women. I guess they were the ones who spent all the money. Admittedly, I wasn't much of a shopper, but I liked to look at antique guns and coins. There was a really cool shop I stumbled into where this ancient gentleman sold all kinds of items he'd created himself carved out of wood he'd found. Some of it was driftwood, other was pine and oak. I was instantly smitten. I'd always had a soft spot for people who had a knack for this type of thing and wished I'd learned how to do something like this. Only I was raised by a sadistic bastard whose only intent was beating the shit out of me and when he was tired of that, he'd move on to raping my foster sister, Midnight.

The sounds that came from her room at night still haunted my dreams. She was living the happy life now, but God only knows how she survived. I had more admiration for her than I did most of the people I knew. I would never forgive myself for allowing him to do that to her, even though he would've killed me had I tried to stop him. When the son of a bitch died in prison, it was the best news I'd ever received. Apparently, word had gotten out he was a child molester and prisoners have a certain code. Child molesters don't generally fare well behind bars. My father met a horrid demise and earned what was coming to him.

I stared at a wooden train set on display in the window, one I would've loved to have had when I was a kid. It sat on a matching wooden track and was painted to resemble the local railway trains I'd seen on some of the signs around here.

"Can I help you?"

I turned to see the old man standing behind me. He'd left his carving station to come and assist me.

"Did you create this masterpiece?" I asked.

"Sure did." He smiled with pride.

"It's amazing. The detail is fantastic. How did you learn this?"

"A lot of wood and scars," he said, chuckling. He held up his hands as evidence. Sure enough, there were nicks all over the place.

"You have amazing talent."

"Why, thank you."

"I would've treasured this as a kid."

"Most want computer games now," he said with a sad tinge in his voice. His pained expression matched his tone and I hadn't thought of it before, but he was right. Technology had taken over and kids didn't have the imagination to play with these types of toys anymore.

"I suppose you're right. But this big kid would love nothing more than to have something like this. Is it for sale?"

"I'm sorry to say it isn't. It's a representation of our town, so to speak. You may not be aware, but Drummond used to be a railroad hub in its heyday. That was before trucking took most of the business away. Anyway, I'm sort of becoming nostalgic."

"Not at all. It's historical, I know. I plan to visit the railroad museum later."

"Excellent. You'll enjoy our little piece of history then. I do have some other carvings you may be interested in though. Do you have an interest in wildlife?"

"Sure. What do you have?"

He showed me some amazing ducks and fish, which of course I purchased. The fish were brightly painted and would look great hanging on a wall. When I was finished paying, I asked about a restaurant recommendation for lunch.

"Since you're headed to the museum, I highly recommend The Depot Cafe. They have the best food in town."

"Great. I'll go there after I tour the museum then. Thanks so much."

I headed to my truck to drop off my items and then went to the museum. It wasn't large by any means but was filled with all sorts of information. I was amazed by how important the railroads were back then. Our nation depended on them. They were its lifeblood and opened up the west for development. But as the auto industry took over and fuel became more available, the trucking industry slowly bled into their profits. They still hold a place today, but not nearly as large as they used to.

When my museum tour was over, I headed next door to what was the old train depot. When I entered the building, my nose was teased with aromas that instantly had my stomach growling. Glancing around, I was happy to see the place was reasonably busy, even though the lunch rush hour should've passed by now. It was almost two.

Walking over to the hostess station, I waited to be seated. That was when it happened. A blond-haired beauty with eyes the color of a summer sky came up to me and greeted me. For a moment, all I could do was gawk at her. Her silky golden hair shimmered with every shift of her head and I had to fist my hands to squelch the urge from reaching out and touching it. But her azure eyes had me blinking furiously because all I could do was imagine myself surrounded by the warm waters of the Pacific.

"Table for one?" she asked, smiling.

I slammed my eyes shut like I'd been punched in the pie hole. Why did she have to smile? How could God have created such a perfect human? It was as though sunshine beamed straight from her.

"Sir, are you okay?" Her voice was the sound of angels. I needed to say something, or she'd think I was on a pass from the nut house.

"Uh, yeah," I breathed. "I'm fine. Do you live here?" Jesus, I sounded like a creep.

"Born and raised, only I recently returned."

"Oh? Where were you?"

"Nosy, aren't you?" Her voice held a hint of mischievousness. "But, you would be. Are you an anchor cranker or a bubblehead?"

It was then I realized she saw my Navy baseball hat and I chuckled at her slang. "I'm neither. I'm DEVGRU. And what branch did you serve in or are you still active?"

"No, I was honorably discharged. But I was a jarhead."

"That a fact? And who do I have the pleasure of speaking to?"

"I'm Lee. Lee Marsten. And you?"

"Ruston Garrett. But everyone calls me Rusty." I aimed a thumb up to my auburn hair. "A pleasure, ma'am."

"Likewise. Come on, let me get you seated so you can have the best meal Drummond, Virginia has to offer."

I followed her to a small round table that was set with a crisp white tablecloth and matching napkin. Once I was sitting, she handed me a menu and told me what the special of the day was.

"Mmm, meatloaf is one of my favorites. Is it good?"

"No, it's horrible. We usually serve crummy specials." Then she winked at me. "What would you like to drink?"

"I'll have a beer."

"Let me get you the beer menu. We have a ton." She walked away and then I noticed the slightest limp as she walked. If I wasn't such a pervert and locked onto her ass, I probably would've missed it. She was back with a wooden board covered in paper that listed a huge selection of craft and regular beers.

"Wow, you do carry a lot."

"Yep. We aim to please."

I placed my order and off she went, only to return a few moments later with my drink.

"If you need anything, just stick your hand up. I'm around."

"Hey, is there anything to do around here?"

"You're not in town to visit anyone?"

"No, I'm on leave, so I'm taking in the local flair."

She chuckled. "That's great. We've had a push to bring in outsiders so how did you hear about Drummond?

"The internet. It painted the town in a bit of a different light."

A hearty laugh escaped her and I joined in.

"Yeah, I told the Visitor's Bureau about that. When I saw it the first time I tried to tell them they should tone it down some, but the shops are what they were going for. And I couldn't argue with that. They were on target. The nightlife was a bit misleading though. Where are you staying?"

"I'm at The Dreamer's Inn."

"Oh, I've heard that's the best place in town. You should enjoy that."

"I haven't checked in yet."

She smiled. "It's one of Drummond's finest. Unless, of course, you prefer the chain hotels."

"To be honest, I can sleep just about anywhere. After spending the night in some less than ideal places and then sleeping on military transport planes, any hotel would suit."

"Yeah, you Seals are pretty tough, or so I'm told." She smirked at me.

"We're a helluva a lot tougher than you jarheads." I poked my tongue into my cheek and waited for her response. But she suddenly was solemn and didn't jump on my comment. "Hey, I didn't mean to offend you."

"No offense taken. It's just that … never mind. My brain went someplace it shouldn't have. Your food should be out momentarily. Enjoy the beer."

She made rounds to some of the other tables and then disappeared behind a swinging door. I was drawn to her. More than I should've been, and I wanted to see her again.

Besides her delivering my meatloaf. It struck me as funny when I thought about it.

I could imagine Midnight and I talking on the phone.

"You met anyone interesting lately?"

"As a matter of fact, I have."

"Oh, who is she?"

"Her name is Lee."

"That's great, Rusty. How'd you two meet?"

"Over my meatloaf."

Her husband would give me so much shit because he would assume the worst about the meatloaf. Jesus. What a conversation starter.

Moments later, I was digging into said meatloaf, and that shit was melting on my tongue. I don't know what the chef did to this stuff, but they should rename it to crackloaf.

Lee stopped by my table to check on me and her brow lifted. "I see you didn't enjoy your special of the day."

"No, you were right. It was horrible. What do you all put in that stuff? It was really something. And those mashed potatoes. I could eat the whole pot."

"You really don't want to know. If you have any plans for working out while you're here, you'd better increase your time by doubling it."

I raised my hand in a salute. "Thanks for the advice. I have a question. Would you by any chance be free tonight?"

Clearly, she wasn't expecting that because her jaw sagged open.

"Uh, why?"

"I was wondering if you'd be interested in giving this lonely soldier a tour of your cozy little town."

Chapter Ten

L<small>EE</small>

"ARE YOU GONNA GO?" Jackson asked.

I chewed on a nail. "Do you think I should?"

"Seriously. Did you look at the man? Tall, built like a brick wall, and sexy as hell. Those freaking eyes. Did you look at those green eyes of his? And his face. Square jaw, perfectly shaped nose, and full lips. What more could a girl want? And oh, my God. Sexy. Did I say sexy?"

"Yes, you said sexy, dammit. Several times. But …"

"But what?"

"You know."

"Oh, come on, Lee. If anyone gives a shit about you, he won't give a damn that you're missing a foot. One foot doesn't make an individual. It's what's in here"—she slammed a hand to her chest—"and here"—and she aimed an index finger to her temple—"that counts."

"Yeah, yeah. I'm just scared. And you know how fragile I am."

"Fragile, my ass. You're the strongest woman I've ever met. Call him. You said you would."

I needed to divert Jackson's attention, so I motioned to the computer. "What do you think about these?" I asked, because the truth was I was shaking in my britches.

Jackson walked behind me as I worked on the flyer I planned to distribute around town. Her silence unnerved me.

"Well?" I asked as I glanced at her over my shoulder.

"I don't know."

"What do you like about it?" I asked.

"How the cafe stands out among the text."

"What don't you like?"

One arm crossed over her chest while the other elbow rested on it. She leaned her chin on the hand that was in the air and thought for a minute. "I don't think the text is a true representation of the cafe."

"Got it." I deleted what I had and redid it, using a different font. "How's this?"

Watching her, her eyes lifted and brightened. "Perfect."

I finished it up and loaded it on my thumb drive. "Gotta go. I have occupational therapy today." This was part of my rehab that was included in what I called my package. "I promised Scuttlebutt he could go with me. I think he's bored not being in school for the summer. I'll get these printed ASAP."

"Awesome. And Lee, I can't thank you enough."

"Hey, I'm kind of like Scuttlebutt. I need something to do too. Laters."

My brother was waiting for me as I pulled into the driveway and he ran out to the car. Occupational therapy was in the next town over, a much larger one than Drummond. We had to drive past the train station and as we did, my brother wanted to know why I was spending so much time there.

"I'm helping Jackson out. I work there now."

"But you can get a better job than that."

"Can I tell you a story?" I asked. "Mom told it in the car on the way home from the airport, but you were listening to your music, so I doubt you heard it."

"Sure."

I launched into the one about our great-grandfather. I wished I hadn't been driving. When you told Scuttlebutt an interesting tale, his eyes saucered like the moon. And I knew when I finished I would be peppered with questions.

"Why didn't he fly?"

"No one did back then. Think about your history, Scutt. Commercial airliners didn't become popular or affordable for that matter until way after World War II."

"Oh, yeah. So where was his family? Didn't anyone care about him?"

"Sure they did. But times were different. His daddy had died, and his mom lived way out in the country and had his younger brothers and sisters to worry about. But here's the coolest thing about what he did. Since there was no one to meet *him*, after he fully recovered, he went to that train station every day until he felt the last soldier had come home just so every one of them would have somebody to greet them when they walked off that train."

Scuttlebutt was super quiet for the longest time, which was very unlike him. Then he started bursting with words that stunned me with their brilliance.

"Lilou, you and Jackson are going about this cafe thing in the wrong way."

"What do you mean?"

"You gotta tell her to change it."

"Why?"

"Look at you. Look at Great-Granddaddy."

I wanted to laugh because he was using the term like we'd known the man intimately, even though we'd never met him.

"Your point?"

"You both had the same things happen to you. You should tie that together and use it for the cafe theme. I think you should change the name of it. The Depot Cafe is too boring. It's not catchy. No pizazz. Every old train station probably has one. Jackson should change it to I'll Be Waiting."

This kid was a genius. "You may have something there, but I have to run it by Jackson because it is her place."

"Lee, you should see if the newspaper would do an article on you and Great-Granddaddy."

"Oh, Scutt, that's a great idea, but I don't know if they'd be interested in something like that."

"I can't think why they wouldn't."

We drove on and arrived at the therapy place. My brother was totally invested in this cafe thing and barely paid attention to what I had to do. He nodded and hummed every now and again, but his brain was buzzing. When he didn't talk, I knew he was doing a lot of thinking, especially since a video game wasn't anywhere in sight.

We got in the car and were headed home when he asked, "Can we stop at the cafe? To talk to Jackson?"

Dang, this kid was totally into this. "If you want."

We swung by and the place was empty. She'd closed for the day. It would be great if her business was ready to sustain the dinner hour and she could stop serving breakfast.

Having heard the door open, Jackson greeted us. "Hey!" She grinned when she saw my brother. "How was therapy?"

"Great. Only a few more and I'm out of jail," I said. "Listen, this kiddo here has something he wants to run by you. He's not sure if you'll think it's worth anything but then again, you never know."

"What is it?"

And my brother proceeded to tell Jackson of his ideas. I beamed with pride at the way he laid out the entire plan. He didn't randomly spit out bits and pieces of information but gave her the story, where he was coming from, and why he thought it would boost the cafe up in the eyes of potential customers. He also was very tactful in the way he approached the name change.

"So, it's not like *The Depot Café* isn't really cool, because it is. But maybe if you added something else to it, like *I'll Be Waiting*, it might jazz it up some."

"So what do you think?" I asked.

"Oh, and one more thing," Scuttlebutt interrupted. "You need press."

We both looked at him and wanted to chuckle.

"Press?" Jackson asked.

"Yeah. You need the paper to cover this place."

"Dude, I know you mean well, but how are we gonna get the paper interested in a cafe?" Jackson asked.

Little bro curled his hand, blew on his fingernails, and rubbed them on his chest. "Don't worry. I got connections."

"I have connections," I corrected.

Scuttlebutt looked at me and asked, "You do?"

"No, I was correcting your grammar."

He looked at the ceiling as though he was begging for intervention. "I'm trying to help you and you're correcting my grammar."

"So, who are these connections?" I asked dubiously, moving him off the grammar topic.

"My friend, Charlie Ammons. His dad works at the paper. I'll ask him about it."

Jackson pinched her lower lip. "So, I'll Be Waiting, huh? How about *I'll Be Waiting,* and then in smaller letters below it *at The Depot Café?*"

"Yeah, that's awesome. It has a much better ring than *The Depot Café*. Don't you think?" little bro asked.

"I have to agree. It doesn't stand out."

"I suppose you're right. Okay, let's do it. That means we need to get our sign changed," Jackson said.

"And we need some old-timey pictures of soldiers back in World War II at train stations and then maybe more recent ones. They may be harder to find because eventually, people started flying."

Scuttlebutt piped in, "And you can also throw in any old picture of people meeting others getting off the train."

"Good point," I said. "I'll start searching online. Oh, and maybe we should do a Grand Re-Opening. Really work this thing to the max, you know? So let's see how long it will take to get it all in order before we decide on a date."

Jackson stood there, her hazel eyes turning warm and golden. "How can I thank you two. This is so … well, it's just great and I can't tell you enough how much I appreciate it. But one thing, I may be in a bit of trouble if it costs too much."

My gray matter whirled as an idea took shape and manifested. "Look, do you want a business partner?"

She cocked her head and asked, "What do you mean?"

"I have extra money. I can partner with you. Not a fifty-fifty deal because you're doing the chef work and all, but maybe twenty-five seventy-five. I can help you out now with whatever you need, and we can draw up a contract. This way, you won't feel so overwhelmed by your debt."

"You would do that?" she asked.

"I am already emotionally invested in this place. I may as well be financially invested too."

Jackson held out her hand and said, "I'll only do it under one condition."

"What's that?"

"You call Rusty and accept his offer for a date tonight."

Chapter Eleven

MY PHONE RANG as I was just about to nod off. I had checked into the inn and settled into my room. The big lunch I ate made me somewhat lethargic, so I had walked around town some more but decided a nap was in order. It was late afternoon, so I decided it was time to go to the inn.

"Hello?"

"Rusty, this is Lee."

Her voice instantly perked me up.

"Hey, Lee. I didn't think you'd call."

"Sorry it took a while. I had therapy this afternoon and I'm just getting home. My answer is yes. What would you like to do?"

"Maybe you should decide since you're the hometown girl."

A soft laugh hit my ears. "Honestly, that doesn't leave a

whole lot of options. But I'll meet you at the inn and we'll go from there. Does that sound okay?"

"Sounds great. How's six?"

"I'll see you then."

I had an hour to get ready. I should've asked her what to wear, but this seemed like a casual town, so I was fairly certain jeans would be in order. It better be because that's all I brought.

Right before six, I went to the lobby of the inn and waited. When she walked in, it was as though someone let the sunshine in. She wore a simple black tank top that exposed her lovely shoulders, along with a pair of jeans. I loved her in jeans. They showed off her ass very nicely.

"Hey," she said.

"Wow, you look great."

She winked at me. "That's quite a compliment coming from someone like you."

Her comment puzzled me. "What do you mean?"

"Aren't you supposed to give me hell since I was a marine?" she asked.

"I think I'll make an exception this time. Besides, why would I want to give hell to such a gorgeous woman like yourself?"

Her lips formed a perfect O and it took all sorts of restraint not to press my own to hers. I remembered how Harrison once told me that when he first met Midnight, the attraction was so potent he couldn't stop thinking about her. This was exactly what I was experiencing toward Lee.

"Shall we?" I offered her my arm and we left. I slammed the door behind me and she jerked so hard I thought she left the ground.

"You okay?" I asked.

"Yeah. Loud noises still affect me from being over there, you know?"

"I understand. I shouldn't have slammed the door so hard."

"Hey, don't make excuses. It's my problem, not yours. I'm much better than I was when I first got back."

My truck, which was parked in the lot, wasn't difficult to miss. "I hope you don't mind riding in a truck."

"Not at all. But since you have no idea where you're going, it's probably best if I drive. Besides, I have something planned for us."

"Sounds great." We walked to a Honda Accord that was parked a few spots down from my truck. I held her door open and then I got in.

"I thought I'd give you a tour of the area and then take you to a favorite place of mine."

"This is a great idea," I said. "You're my personal tour guide."

She drove away and pointed to several landmarks that dotted the scenery. "There truly isn't much to Drummond, but it's a cozy little town and was a wonderful place to grow up."

"So how did you end up working in the restaurant."

"Oh, that's easy."

She explained about her friend from high school who became a chef and came back and opened up the cafe. "That's a great story."

But then her excitement grew as she told me about the new plans they made only today for the future and their new joint venture.

"How awesome for you."

After a quick sidelong glance at me, her eyes were back on the road. "Yeah, well, I had planned on making a career out of the marines. I really loved that life. But, things didn't quite work out that way. When I got back here, the restaurant had opened, only I didn't know it was Jackson who'd owned it. I was super excited for her. We were best friends in high school but had lost touch over the years. It's a win-win for the two of us."

"Sounds like it. Can I ask you what happened that took you out of the marines?"

"It was an IED."

"Ah, fuck. I'm sorry, Lee."

"I may as well fill you in. I'm an amputee."

"No shit."

She laughed humorlessly. "No shit. Call me stumpy."

"Oh, you think you're funny."

"Not really," she said. She ran a finger around the edge of the steering wheel.

"Good, because that shit isn't funny one bit."

"No, it's not. I came pretty close to dying. I lost the lower part of one leg and came damn close to losing the other."

Even though the gesture was far more intimate than our relationship called for, I rested my hand on her thigh. I'm terribly sorry. I can't imagine going through anything close to that. We face it all the time, but for it to really happen ..." I can only shake my head.

"Thank you. I'm much better than at the beginning. I cursed a lot. My physical therapists—whew, did they ever put up with some seriously bad language."

"Hey, you're in the military. They should've expected it. But looking at you now, you don't give me that impression, Lee."

"Yeah, when I knew I'd be coming home, I had to clean up my act. My little brother is very impressionable and that wouldn't have set a very good example."

"Little brother?"

"Yeah. His name is Glenn, but I call him Scuttlebutt because he can't sit still for anything and always has the latest news in town. He's really an amazing kid and I adore him."

"How old is he?"

"He's fourteen and adorable."

Suddenly, I'm back to being fourteen again and I can hear my asshole of a father screaming at me, throwing a gut punch to me because I didn't fold a towel perfectly, or maybe it was because the hose in the yard hadn't been coiled correctly. I carried so many bruises every day from him that I could barely walk and stand up straight.

"Rusty? Earth to Rusty? You with me?"

"Oh, sorry."

"Where'd you go?"

"Someplace you don't ever want to be."

"Why's that?"

"It's just a place filled with bad memories. I'm glad your little brother has you as a big sister and friend."

"Did I tell you he was instrumental in some of the plans for the restaurant?" And then she explained.

"It sounds like your little Scuttlebutt is going to be an entrepreneur someday."

"I think so."

After Lee showed me several more places of interest, she drove a short distance out of town and then pulled off the road where there was an old covered bridge.

"Well, look at this."

"Pretty cool, huh?"

"I'll say."

"There's a really neat creek below with some minuscule rapids where the water dances over the rocks. You can hang out and splash in the water and it's also fun to fish here too. Do you like to fish?"

"I love it. I think Drummond is a special place."

"It is. Let's go."

She got out of the car and went to the trunk. Inside were a blanket, cooler, and a picnic basket.

"Here's my surprise. We're going to picnic on the covered bridge."

"Nice," I said. "This is a first for me." I carried everything but the blanket, but when she had the perfect spot picked, I spread the blanket out for us.

She pulled out a bag that contained plenty of candles, which she set around us and lit. "Just so you know, Jackson put this together. She thinks of everything."

"Nice. I need to thank her."

"Yeah, I'm surprised she didn't sit in your lap earlier today and hug you for flirting with me."

"Is that a fact?"

"Yes. She thinks I take life far too seriously."

"The military does that to some people. It makes others far too reckless."

"Yeah, I can see that. So, tell me about yourself. Why the Seals?"

"It sort of just happened. I was this scrawny kid growing up. Helpless and bullied in school. My old man used me as his punching bag and beat the shit out of me every day. Or if not every day, every other day."

"Oh, God, Rusty, I'm sorry."

The sun has set, so it's too dark now to tell for sure, but somehow I knew her eyes were filled with sorrow for me. But not pity. I didn't want her pity. And I knew for damn sure she didn't want mine.

"It's in the past from a long time ago and the bastard is dead now so …"

"Yeah, but those kinds of scars never go away, and no

one should have to endure that kind of crap. I hate that for you."

"Thank you. But somehow, it made me strong. Strong enough to survive SEAL training."

"Damn. And I hear that BUD/S is a cruel bitch."

"You can say that again. I didn't think I'd ever warm up again."

"I've heard stories."

"So, yeah, when the call went out, I thought, what the hell. What do I have to lose? And damn if I didn't make it."

"But Team Six?"

I shrugged. This is really an off-limits topic for me. "Yeah, well, it's just a designation. DEVGRU is what I was assigned to. It's a unit in the military like any other."

She scoffed. "You might be able to pull that bullshit line on other civilians, but you can't do that to me. I've seen some of your squadrons in action. Or I should say I've seen the aftermath of what you guys can do and you are not the average soldier."

I ran a hand through my hair. "Sure, I'll give you that. Our training is impeccable, and we are highly specialized. But unlike the rest of the military, we've spent months and months doing this. It was intense and swear to God, most of us have near-death experiences doing it."

"I get that. But take the credit for it."

"Okay. Now, can we change this touchy subject? This is pretty much an off-limits discussion, you know."

"Yeah, I do. Sorry."

"Not a problem. Besides, I'm starving and dying to see what you have in your little box of tricks over there."

That got a good chuckle out of her and it diverted her attention, so she went about digging into the cooler and presented me with a drink.

"Thank you." I popped the beer open with the opener she handed me. "That's the only thing I dislike about these fancy beers. They don't have the twist off caps."

"Yeah, but I think they're cool."

The candlelight caught her smile and her beauty charmed me. The first thing that came to mind popped out of my mouth. "Were you not constantly hit on when you served?"

"What?"

"I mean, you are so damn beautiful."

A hand flew to her hair and she smoothed it. "Please don't."

"Don't what? Tell the truth?"

"Yes, no. I don't know."

"Then what?"

Her eyes blazed holes through me.

"Wait. Don't tell me it's because of your foot?" When she didn't answer, I plowed on. "If you think for one second just because you're missing a foot that I'm going to somehow think lesser of you, then you don't know me very well. But then again, you don't know me at all. We just met. So, I'm going to do my damnedest to prove to you I'm not that kind of guy. And don't even think about not letting me because I'm an obstinate motherfucker. Now, are you gonna feed me or let me starve to death here?"

Chapter Twelve

Lee

THE CORNERS of my mouth tugged upward. Him starving was one thing that was never going to happen— not when he was in my company anyway. I scrambled to fix him a plate of the best potato salad a human being could create, and then I added a chicken salad croissant, along with some mixed fruit salad that contained a mixture of watermelon and freshly grated coconut. The plate was so heavy I was afraid the dang thing was going to split in half.

When I handed it to him, I said, "Make sure you keep a hand on the bottom."

He did and thanked me. Then I made one for myself, only didn't load it near as full. After his first few bites, he hummed his delight and managed to let me know how tasty everything was.

"I was going to ask you because you didn't say anything."

"I'm having a food orgasm."

"I didn't think men had those," I said.

"Who told you that?"

"No one. I just thought it because men don't talk about food like women do."

"You're not hanging out with the right men."

"Nice to know."

He went back to his food and the man didn't come up for air until his plate was completely empty. "I have more if you want," I announced.

"Please," he said, looking like a little kid waiting on candy. I gave him a refill and watched him go to town. The guy could pack it away. It was nice watching someone enjoy their food and not worry about putting on weight. I had to be careful because of my prosthesis. If I gained much weight, the thing might get too tight or it could also be too uncomfortable for me as far as the pressure on the stump.

We both finished at about the same time.

"Can I get you another beer?" I asked.

"How about I get one myself. And do you need anything?"

"No thanks, I'm fine."

He grabbed another out of the cooler and settled back down. "That was some of the best food I've ever had."

"And what was the best?"

"That meatloaf I had for lunch."

"Really?"

"Truth. I don't eat much home cooking, but that was a list topper."

"You don't cook then?" I asked.

"A little, if you count frozen dinners and bagged salad. I can do some stuff on the grill."

"Like what?"

"Ribs."

"I love ribs."

"Then I'll have to cook you some."

"So, when did you get back to Drummond?"

I tuck the hair back around my ear. "Been back around a month now."

He surprised me when he grabbed my hand. His was strong and warm, but it was also the hand of a man who did hard work. It was calloused and rough, but he held mine with a gentle touch.

"What was it like? Coming home I mean?"

"Weird. Everything was the same, but different."

His thumb began making circles over my own. "How so?"

I pinched my nose for a second. "It was like the town had been shaded a different hue. After I got hit, I was in a bad place for a while. My shrink had to jerk me around a bit to make me realize I was lucky to be breathing air and not eating dirt. I was hardheaded and unwilling to accept this." I lifted and pointed to my leg. "Bitterness was my best friend, or so I thought. Until Marianna Perez, my shrink, jerked a knot in my panties. She was tough on me for all the right reasons."

"And what were those reasons?"

"That day we were on patrol, I was the one who spotted the IED, and thank God I saw it." I explained what happened. "If I hadn't suspected it, the entire team would've been injured, or worse yet, killed. I prevented some injuries and she helped me realize that. So this"—I held up my prosthesis and knocked on it with my fist—"is a small price to pay for the lives of my fellow soldiers."

"I hope this doesn't offend you, and I apologize in advance if it does."

I was confused by his comment until his two arms

wrapped around me and lifted me onto his lap. Then his mouth sought out mine and he kissed me. I had never been kissed so thoroughly before. He wasn't tentative one bit. This man knew exactly what he wanted and he went right after it. One hand held my hip steady while the other framed my cheek. His tongue licked the seam of my mouth, then pressed through the opening until it met my own. Once there, it mingled with mine, sending all sorts of delicious waves of pleasure dancing down my spine until a wave of butterflies fluttered in my belly.

I breathed his name, winding my arms around his neck, which only had him deepen the kiss. My pulse was racing and I wondered if his was too. When he broke off the kiss, he smiled and buried his hand in my hair.

"Beautiful Lee. I'm sorry if that kiss offended you, but it's easier to ask forgiveness later than beg for permission. I stole that quote from somewhere and sorry if I don't remember where, but I like it." He offered up a sheepish grin and I laughed.

"I'm glad you kissed me and there's nothing to forgive. I quite liked it."

"Than that means I'll have to kiss you some more."

And he did. I'd never been made to feel like this by a mere kiss, but then Rusty wasn't a mere man. He seemed special somehow. Honest with integrity. How did I know this? I didn't really. But I felt it deep down in my heart.

His mouth moved from mine and kissed the corner of my lips. Then it trailed across my cheek to the column of my neck where his tongue tickled me for a bit until his mouth turned sensual once again and his teeth lightly nipped my skin. I was writhing against him, wanting more. It had been ages since I had been with a man. The truth was, I had given up any ideas of ever being with one again.

I didn't think anyone would want a disfigured woman, but Rusty made me forget about that.

As those thoughts flitted through my head, he lifted me over his lap to straddle his hips. Then we were eye to eye as he seated me on top of him. He wanted me. I could feel the steel length of him under his jeans.

"It's no secret, is it?" he asked, reading my mind.

"That's sort of hard to hide, no pun intended."

His body shook as he laughed.

"I didn't intend to go there."

"Uh, it's been a really long time for me, Rusty. And after Afghanistan, I never thought …"

"Never thought what?"

I shrugged.

"Don't tell me the leg thing again."

I looked away before I responded. "Most guys don't want a woman who's disfigured."

"Maybe not the shallow ones. And do you know what I say to that?"

"What?"

"I'm glad because that puts me at the front of the line."

I fake punched him in the shoulder. "You're crazy."

"I know. For you."

"You just met me."

"You see, my foster sister's husband once told me that he pretty much knew right at the beginning she was the one for him."

"So what are you saying?"

He ran his hand through his cropped hair. "I think that's how I feel about you. And no, I don't want to run off with you right now or anything, but there's something about you that just clicks with me. I don't usually feel like this with women. And I don't go around saying this kind of stuff to women either. And I'm not trying to fuck you or anything. Christ, I have the shits of the mouth tonight."

"I think it's adorable. Go on."

He picked up a chunk of my hair and twirled it around his finger. "I'm fairly guarded with my words and emotions. My upbringing wasn't the best as you've heard. So I guess my point here is I think perhaps we should explore this thing, whatever it is, between us. If it happens to turn into something huge, which I think it will, then we can decide what to do later. So what's your opinion?"

"I agree. There's something about you, Rusty, that clicks with me too. So I'm all in. But I have a question. Where do you live?"

"Virginia Beach, which isn't too far."

"Only a little over an hour."

"And I still am away a lot, so we can visit when I'm home. Maybe you can come and stay with me," he said.

"Would you want that?"

"No. Not at all. I wouldn't want to see you or spend any time with you, Lee." He gave me a smart-ass grin. "The fact is, at some point, I'd want to spend an entire week, or maybe a month in bed with you."

"Well, we would have to eat. And then you do have to cook me ribs sometime." I licked my lips.

"The grill is on the deck right off the bedroom. I'll figure something out. Maybe purchase some super long tongs. I could flip them from the bed," he said, laughing.

"Do you always have an answer for everything?"

"I do now, but I didn't when I was a kid."

The creases between his brows are so deep I immediately try to ease them with my fingers. "I'm sorry you have to live like that."

"So am I, but I don't have to anymore. And things are looking even better since I have you in my life."

"I'm gonna call you Speedy."

"Speedy?" He gave me an odd look.

"Yeah, because you're a fast mover."

He waggled his brows and said, "You ain't seen nothing yet, babe."

Chapter Thirteen

RUSTY

HER COMMENT about me being a fast mover wasn't right. I was quite the opposite. But with her, everything was different. *She* was different. Where my world was dark and murky, filled with storm clouds and doom, she represented brightness and sunshine, joy and laughter. I'd never experienced anything like her before. My life hadn't offered me much of that until she walked into it. And I was going to make it my goal to win her over. Yeah, I'd only just met her. Yeah, this was fast. Really fast. But I already knew Lee Marston was mine. She was meant for me just as I was for her. Maybe she didn't know it yet, but she would soon.

After our dinner had ended and we moved from under the covered bridge, we gazed at the sky painted with stars.

"Have you ever felt like this was placed here just to make us feel small somehow?" she asked.

"What do you mean?"

"Look at how vast it is." She swept her arm across the space before us. "We're like ants in comparison."

"I believe God has a great sense of humor."

"In which way?" she asked.

I picked up her arm and repeated her motion. "That vastness is of such great magnitude, he wants to tease us with it every night with its beauty. Humans have a tendency to believe we are so advanced … to think we have such brilliant technology. But yet look at what's beyond us … what we don't know … or can't touch. God is dangling that carrot in front of us."

"But why?"

I shrugged. "Who's to say? Maybe to make believers out of all of us. It's hard to deny that this"—I extended my arm out this time—"had to come from somewhere. Oh, I know. The Big Bang Theory and all. But that original particle had to originate from somewhere. And why can't that coincide with God's creation?"

"You're preaching to the choir here. When I was in and out of it after the explosion, I saw all kinds of things that only confirmed my belief."

"I lost all my faith in God when I was a kid living in the hell I grew up in." Flashes of my father's face nailed me in the sternum, and I sucked in air.

Her hand touched my thigh and she asked, "Hey, are you okay?"

I snorted with disgust. "I am now. But back then …" my voice trailed off.

"Do you want to talk about it?"

"Generally, I'd say no. It's not something I ever talk about except on rare occasions, but with you, I feel different. My old man was basically a monster. He had his hands into all sorts of criminal activities, but the one that sent him behind bars was an illegal porn ring. He got mixed up with this group where they'd drug women and then video them having sex. Those videos would be sold on a porn hub afterward."

"That's awful."

"My foster sister testified against him because she was one of the women he had drugged and raped."

"Wait, are you serious? He did this to his own foster kid?"

"He raped her constantly while she lived with us. She ended up getting pregnant and running away. It was a tragic situation, all the way around. Her life was worse than mine. Her mom had passed and then she landed with us, only to find herself stuck with a vile animal like my father. I wanted to help her so much, but he threatened me. Told me he'd kill me if I opened my mouth or tried to intervene. Back then I didn't weigh a hundred pounds."

"Jesus. That's … I don't have any words for what that must've been like."

I rub my head because this is the part I hate the most. "Here's the worst. She came to me, begging to run away with her. I mentioned going to the police, but she didn't want that because she said they'd send us into foster care. The idea freaked her out since she was living in a hell. Now that I truly understand what she'd been facing, I get it. But then I thought the cops would help. The system had to have been so broken that there were people like my parents who were able to get through. I'm not sure how it is today. I can only pray it's better. She feared she'd land into another home like ours. So she ran and I stayed. She made it though. She turned eighteen and was free. When I turned eighteen, I left too and joined the Navy. That was my ticket to freedom. But to this day, the guilt still eats at me about not going with her."

"But why? You just said she made it."

"She did. But the baby she had didn't. He died of a rare congenital heart defect. And she was all alone to bear that by herself. Had I been with her, I could've helped her get through that."

"Oh, Rusty, you were still a kid. You didn't know. Couldn't have known. If there is anyone to blame, it's your father. He was the one that caused all the pain. It wasn't you."

Smiling sadly, I said, "Yeah, I tell that to myself all the time, but it doesn't help much. Knowing that my sister is happy and is married now and has two healthy kids makes me happy. She doesn't blame me either."

"I wouldn't expect her to. Where is she now?"

"Oh, I didn't tell you?"

"No."

"My foster sister is Midnight Drake."

Her mouth silently says the name and out loud she asked, "The movie star?"

"Uh huh."

"That's your sister?"

"Yep."

"Oh my God. I remember now hearing about her when she went to court. But that was a few years ago and I was on my first tour, so I was getting the information sort of piecemeal."

"Yeah. She's the one who brought my dad down and then I also testified against him."

"Wow. That must've been some trial. And your mom?"

"She died shortly after I left home. She was a bad alcoholic. She was aware of what he did because she got her share of beatings too. I imagine the alcohol was her way of dealing with him."

She grabbed my hand and laced our fingers together.

"I can't imagine living like that. My family is so normal and loving."

"You should appreciate that and never ever take that for granted."

Squeezing our locked fingers, she said, "You're right. I never have and never will. Family is everything."

She drove me back to the inn that night and I held her hand the whole way home. "Tell me this isn't too much."

"What?" she asked.

"You and me. I've talked your ear off, telling you things you may not have been ready to hear. I hope I didn't freak you out."

After she parked the car, she swiveled a bit to face me. I relaxed a bit when her hand touched my cheek. "I think we're good."

"Just good?"

She laughed and it was a great sound. It was bubbly like a child's when they got excited over something. "Okay, we're great."

"Now you sound like Tony the Tiger in the Frosted Flakes commercial."

"Oh my God. How's this? We're exceptional."

"Much better. And I'm not Speedy. Never have been in the past anyway."

"No?"

I slowly shook my head. "But there's just something about you, Lee, that's hit me."

"How so?"

I cupped a hand to her neck and drew her closer. "I want to be close to you. In many ways." Then I kissed her and it was the sweetest honey I'd ever tasted. I gained satisfaction from the fact that she returned my kiss. "But not just this. It's more than this."

"Tell me."

I took her hand and kissed her knuckles. "I'm not sure if I can. It's in here." I laid her palm over my heart. "You're probably thinking I'm super weird now."

"No, not at all. I want to be close to you too. When I saw you walk into the cafe today, I felt you were different. But ever since the explosion, I've been wary of … well, you know. So I didn't expect anything."

It takes all my self-control not to pull her across the seat and put her in my lap. "Maybe you were only waiting."

"Waiting?"

I lower my voice and say, "Waiting for me … for the right one."

Her hand flies over her mouth.

"Is that so difficult to believe?"

"No. It's not that. It's something else. My great-grandparents. You won't believe this."

Chapter Fourteen

LEE

WHEN I FINISHED the story about how my great grand-parents met, Rusty grabbed my hips and pulled me onto his lap.

"Do you believe in destiny?" he asked in a rush.

"I don't know. I never really thought about it."

"Think about it for a second. Their story and now ours. The two of us meeting at the cafe. Doesn't it sound a bit more than coincidental? Why else would I have come to Drummond? It's not exactly a huge tourist hub and when I found it online, I wondered myself why I made that reservation."

"But the railroad museum," I protest.

"Sure, I liked trains as a kid, but I haven't thought about them in years. It's not like I actively seek out these kinds of places. I'm not a homey town kind of guy. In fact, I hid this from my buddies. If they found out where I spent part of my leave, I'd never hear the end of it. It didn't make much sense to me, but I didn't have anything else to do so I figured, what the hell."

He did have a point. A huge glaring one. Single men weren't flocking to Drummond in droves by any means.

"Okay, score one for Rusty. But coincidences happen all the time."

"Yeah, they do. But not like this. Say we met, and then that was that. But Lee, it wasn't just a meet and greet, how ya doin', and adios. I don't want to leave the day after tomorrow. I want to see you every day. I want to talk to you every day. The thought of going back to Virginia Beach is making me itchy. That's not normal. And my instincts … I live and die by them."

"Okay, score two for Rusty. I'm not exactly happy about you leaving either."

"And then we have the meeting place. If we'd met passing on the street, or in a different restaurant, or even in that tiny museum, I'd say, maybe coincidence, but come on. You have to give some credibility to what I'm saying here. Great grandma and great grandpa are hard at work matchmaking, sweetheart. You can try and deny it all you want, but I'm giving them my blessing and thanking them. And I'm also going back to that little wood shop and thanking the old owner for sending me there."

"What old owner?" I asked.

"You know, the old gentleman who sits in the back and does all the cool wood carving."

"Nope, the only guy in that shop is Neal and he's in his mid-forties."

"Nah, this guy is at least eighty. His hands are all scarred up and everything. I asked if that train set in the window was for sale and he said it wasn't. Then he sold me some other things instead."

"No way. Neal is the only guy in there. He's the shop owner. No one else works there to my knowledge."

"Maybe this was Neal's dad."

"Huh uh. Neal's dad passed about eight years ago."

Rusty scratched his head. "I don't know then, but I swear there was an old guy in there and he told me to go to The Depot Cafe to eat because they had the best food in town.

"Weird. I'll have to check into that tomorrow."

"Me too. But that'll be after my breakfast at the cafe. Which, I'd better let you go because I know you have to work."

"No, Jackson gave me the morning off. I'm to report in at noon."

"Oh, yeah?"

"Oh, yeah." I grinned at him. Jackson had all kinds of ideas, but I wasn't going down that road yet with Rusty, even though I wanted to. I was a bit rusty—haha—and I needed a little more warming up in that regard.

"Care to come to my room, little girl?"

"What are you, the big bad wolf?"

"Not at all. I'm more like a cuddly puppy. And I promise to behave. I swear."

"Ok. Under one condition. I won't sleep with you because this is our first date."

"Lee, I would never pressure you into that. Ever. But, I can't swear I won't kiss you."

"I'm good with that." And I was. Ever since I'd joined the Marines, I'd been one of the guys and it was different being treated like this. Rusty's kisses made my stomach flutter, to the point that I wanted much more with him. He was better than anyone I'd ever been with and he could kiss me as much as he wanted. This would be my little secret. Letting him in on it wasn't an option quite yet.

When he unlocked his door, his hotel room was much nicer than I thought it would be.

"Wow. This place is really great."

"Yeah, I was impressed."

It had a king-sized bed, a huge sitting area, and a giant bathroom with a separate shower.

"How much per night if you don't mind me asking?"

"Only one twenty."

"This is a steal."

"I know. This town should add a few more things to do and it could take off. Especially since it's only a few miles from the main interstate."

"We're hoping." I held up my crossed fingers.

Rusty walked to the small refrigerator and grabbed a couple of beers, handing me one. But before he could pop it open, I impulsively reached for him and pulled his mouth down to mine.

The bottles forgotten, he lifted me higher to align us and took over the kiss. Sliding his tongue against mine, he tickled and teased every part of my mouth until I moaned. Currents of fire soared throughout my veins, and the unexpected idea of tearing his clothes off popped into my mind. I'd never been the aggressor in a relationship before, but surprisingly, I wanted to be that person now. I held back, of course, because I didn't want him to think I was some shameless hussy desperate for a man. I also didn't want to scare him off either.

He broke off the kiss and his piercing gaze penetrated my own. The emotion behind those emerald irises had the oxygen jammed in my lungs. He was right. There definitely was something firing off between us.

"You feel it too, don't you, Lee?"

I swallowed the thick knot that had come out of

nowhere and dipped my head slightly. I couldn't bear to look away from him. "Yeah," I breathed the word.

His legs took us to the bed, for which I was grateful. I wanted to lie in his arms and feel him between my thighs. I wanted to—oh, shit. I had not prepared for this moment at all. I was so adamant about not sleeping with him on the first date that I hadn't bothered to shave or wax. Fuck, fuck, fuck. I groaned.

"What's wrong."

"Nothing. Not a thing."

"It's something. I can tell."

"We're not gonna get naked, are we?"

"Do you want to get naked?"

"Uh, yeah, sort of."

He raised a brow. "Sort of?"

"I might have a slight issue."

"What kind of an issue?"

"Promise you won't laugh."

He was so sincere when he answered that I was the one who almost laughed. "I promise."

"I didn't shave my legs."

For one instant, he looked puzzled, and then he bit down on his lips. It was obvious he was trying his best not to break his promise.

"You promised."

"I know," he murmured between his lips he held together. Then little by little, his body began shaking.

"You're supposed to be a freaking Navy Seal, forced to endure all sorts of torture and you can't even contain your laughter." That did it. He burst out in a huge guffaw, threw his head back on the bed and howled.

Did I mention the man was huge—in comparison to me anyway. He was about six feet two. And solid as a brick wall. I went to play punch him in the gut and my fist came up against steel abs.

"Jeez, Rusty, let me see what you have hiding underneath that shirt. Is it granite or what?" I tugged his shirt until it exposed the smooth flesh of his stomach and found the clearly defined ridges of an eight pack that veered off in both directions to form a perfect V from his obliques. "Good Lord. What kind of a workout do you do?"

"We have the best trainers in the country and we adhere to a rigid physical training program. It's part of the requirement."

"It's obvious. I bet you can do pull-ups, can't you?"

"That's another requirement."

But all talk about physical exercise disappeared when he pushed me on my back and hovered over me. "Now what was all the fuss about not shaving?"

"Er, you may want to close your eyes if we get naked."

"Who said anything about getting naked, Lee?" His voice was hoarse and sent shivers across my flesh.

"I did."

"I think we should take this one step at a time."

"Me too. You kissed me. That was step one. Let's move to step two."

"Which is?" he asked.

"You undress half of me."

"Which half?"

Using both of my thumbs, I pointed to my chest. "This half."

He buried his hand in my hair and said, "I think I'm going to like this step." His lips touched my neck and made their way down to where it joined my shoulder. My fingers sunk into the hard muscle of his arms and his hand slid beneath my tank top.

The idea of him seeing me without my top was fine,

but the part below the waist made me freeze. I grabbed his hand and clamped down.

"What is it?" he asked.

The saliva in my mouth had disappeared and my tongue was scotch taped to the roof of my mouth. Words disappeared and I became mute.

"Lee, are you all right?"

I licked my lips, with a bone-dry tongue, then swallowed. "Um, I'm …" I couldn't tell him. All my bravado was gone.

"What is it? You can trust me."

I knew he was truthful, but yet, no one had seen my leg. Well, only a few people anyway.

"It's just that …"

"Hey, we don't have to do this, you know."

"No, I want to. I'm a little nervous." It was way more than a little, but I didn't want him to know.

He held my hand and helped me take his own shirt off. When I saw what had been hidden underneath, my fingers began a little exploration of their own. The more I explored, the more I relaxed, and the more I wanted this man. My hands reveled in his strength, in the rhythm of his heart beating beneath my fingertips.

"You're perfect," I told him.

"Hardly."

"You are." And he was. He'd told me I was beautiful, but I'd never seen a more gorgeous man.

He leaned away from me and I sat up to get rid of my top and bra. When I was bared from the waist up, he only stared at me.

"Lee. I've never seen anything so lovely." He touched me as though I were a fine piece of china afraid I would break. Gently, he pushed me back and his mouth sucked a nipple inside. My back arched from the sensation. I was flames and fire to his touch. He moved to my other nipple and all I could think of was how I wanted to feel him —all of him. Against me, in me, flesh to flesh, skin to skin.

He released me and moved back to kiss me.

"Lee, I'd like nothing more than to—"

"Yes, I want that too!"

He chuckled. "You don't even know what I was going to say."

"Weren't you going to say you wanted to have sex with me?"

"No, I was going to say I wanted to make love to you before you got a little exuberant there. But"—he held up a finger—"maybe we should wait."

"Why?"

"I want you to be sure."

My heart nudged my ribs. How was I this lucky to have found a guy as considerate as him? "I've been waiting a long time for this and don't think I'm going into this lightly. I'm sure, Rusty."

He laughed again and rolled over, taking me with him. "Are you always this spontaneous?"

"Not really. I haven't been with anyone in ages and never thought I'd find someone I'd want to be with again. Here we are with these crazy as hell feelings going on and even though it's scary as hell, I don't want to wait. You really do?"

"I'm trying to be a gentleman and you're making it hard as hell."

I lifted up my head and said, "Rusty, I don't want you to be a gentleman. I want you to play dirty in bed. But don't hold it against me that I didn't shave." I wrinkled up my nose.

Abruptly, he set me on the bed and stood up.

"Play dirty, huh? You like dirty? I can do dirty. In fact,

dirty is my middle name. Ruston Dirty Garrett, at your service." And then he proceeded to undress, but when he got to the underwear that he didn't wear, I gasped. He was big. Much bigger than I ever expected.

"Whoa."

"Don't fear the beast. He will love you … dirty and diligently."

I didn't think I'd said it out loud. My hand covered my mouth as I laughed. "Oh my God. You did not just say that."

"I did and it's a promise. Now let's get that unshaven body of yours undressed."

In an instant, I was self-conscious again. Not because I hadn't shaved, but because of my prosthesis and scarred leg. My eyes slammed shut and I cringed.

"Hey, what's going on here?"

"Nothing, let's do this."

"Lee, baby, we're not gonna just do this if you don't talk to me."

I opened my eyes to find his green ones right in front of me. My heart stuttered and then beat like the wings of a hummingbird.

"Oh, my. I'm super nervous. I've never let anyone see my legs since the accident."

He gripped my hand and said, "I've seen a lot of shit, and I'm sure your legs aren't bad—maybe in your eyes they are. But I can assure you they won't be in mine. I hate you had to go through that experience. But your legs aren't what define you. It's what's inside of you. We can sit here like this all night if you want. We don't have to go any farther, you know."

"I know, but I honestly want to. I want us to share each other."

"Then tell me what to do."

"Take off my pants."

He followed my directions. When my pants were off, my legs were exposed. To me, the stump and jagged scars weren't a big deal anymore. But to others, I'm sure it must've been horrid to look at. I kept my eyes squeezed shut for fear of what I'd find reflected in his.

His hands were gentle as they touched me. Fingers traced the scars, one by one, on each leg, until he came to the end of the line. "So, do you want to keep your prosthesis on for this?"

"Uh, no. I'll remove it. Is that okay with you?"

"Why would you ask me that?"

"Because you'll have to see my stump."

He cupped my face. "Lee, that's your leg and it won't bother me. Take it off or I can do it for you if you'll tell me what to do."

Oh, Jesus. This man was so sweet. Did he really exist? I took the damn thing off, but still refused to look at him. But I shouldn't have been afraid.

"Was that so bad?"

"Guess not," I answered.

"Lee, you have to look at me."

When I did, the only thing I saw in his eyes was admiration.

"Okay, it wasn't bad at all. Now that I'm naked, can we make the most of it?"

"That is a definite."

But the first thing he went to do almost had me running out the door. That is if I could've run without a leg. He pushed me back until my shoulder blades hit the bed and then he spread my legs. Without a second to be wasted, his mouth fell between my thighs and … oh shit.

"What are you doing?" I nearly screamed.

He lifted his head and said, "What do you think I'm doing?"

"You can't do *that*."

His brow formed some serious creases. "Why not?"

"Well, because."

"That's not an answer."

"Yeah, it is."

"No, it's not." And his mouth dropped back down as I gasped.

"Because I haven't shaved down there. That's why."

His head popped back up and he said, "What's the big deal? Relax and stop overthinking things. I promise you'll love it."

His mouth went back to work, and I didn't have a chance to think about anything except for what his lips and tongue, and then, oh fuck, what his fingers were doing. And just what the hell were they doing? He had one, no two, inside of me, and they were doing some little fancy motion that felt so fucking good. His tongue was flicking my clit in a circular motion and I was about to come. To come like a motherlode.

"Whatever you do, don't you stop. Oh, God, don't stopppppp." I moaned.

My fingers grasped his head, or rather his hair, and I ground my pelvis against his mouth. Then my orgasm started in the arch of my foot and shot straight through to the top of my head. I moaned out, "Ohhhhh, Russsssty. Yesssssssssss." I sounded exactly like the shameless hussy I was. Christ, what would his neighbors at the inn think?

But he didn't take his mouth off me. He kept fingering and flicking me off. I was frenzied with this epic climax he kept giving and giving. My sensitive nub couldn't take any more, so I begged him to stop.

"Please, no more."

He didn't listen. I was practically contorted with my spasms. Then another giant orgasm nailed me and I mewled his name, sounding like the local tomcat. When this one let loose, it left me limp and weak in its wake.

He finally lifted his head, wiped his face with the bed sheet, and announced, "Fuck, that was sexy as hell. You're so damn wet."

Then he stood up and rifled through the contents of his bag to return with a handful of condoms. *A handful.* Jesus, I was a dead woman.

He lifted my knees, spread my legs, and I gawked at him as he rolled on the condom.

"You okay there, babe?" he asked.

"Uh, yeah. Just a bit limp here."

"This'll bring you back to life. Pull your knees to your chest."

I did as he told me and watched as he pushed his long erection into me. Slowly he went, inch by inch, until I was stretched to the max.

"Damn, you're tight." He dropped his head and took my mouth in a searing kiss. While he kissed me, he inched his way out and back in until he was fully seated. "You okay?"

"Yeah. I'm good."

"Let's turn that good into a great, shall we?"

And he started to move. Long and slow even strokes, with my knees still pulled tightly to my chest, and him raised above me, he fucked me like a master.

After a bit, he pulled out and put a pillow on the bed and rolled me on top of it so it was under my hips. Then he slid back inside of me, hitching my hips up. This felt dramatically different in this position. With his hand, he dipped low and rubbed my clit. I was ten seconds from ignition when he said, "I'm going to come, babe. I hope you're close."

"Yes," I whispered, only because I had no breath to spare. My fingers clawed the sheets as the orgasm hit and I moaned and moaned, feeling my inner muscles ripple against him. He held me tightly as he got his own and then collapsed, pulling me into the curve of his body.

"That was perfect, exactly like you are," he murmured in my ear. I hoped he meant it because in one day I had fallen for this man. Weird, but I felt like I'd known him a lifetime.

Chapter Fifteen

LEE

MY PHONE RANG and it woke me up. I glanced around to see Rusty's arm slung over me. "Hello?"

"Lilou Marston?"

"Yes, this is she."

"Ms. Marston, my name is Jeffrey Ammons, and my son is a friend of your brother Glenn's. Glenn spoke with me yesterday about you and your involvement with the cafe in the old train depot. He also told me about your great-grandfather's story and I'd like to do a news story on you and the cafe."

Holy shit!

I sat up, waking Rusty in the process. "Mr. Ammons, this is fantastic. Jackson Blackburn is the owner of the cafe and let me give her a call. It would be great if all three of us could meet. What would be a good time for you?"

He gave me several days and times and I promised I'd

call him back. I immediately called Jackson. She was up to her eyeballs at work.

"Hey Lee. What's up?"

"You won't believe this. That little Scuttlebutt was right!" And I gave her the details.

We decided on the following day, so I called Mr. Ammons back to set it up. In my excitement, I jumped out of bed and forgot to put on my prosthesis. Not a good idea. In my haste, I crashed on my face in zero point two seconds, letting out a loud yell.

"Shit! Shit!"

Rusty was at my side, helping me. "Lee, are you okay?" His hands ran down my leg, checking for injuries, I suppose.

An embarrassed giggle leaked out of me. God, I never giggled, but this was so humiliating. I needed to remember to hop and not run next time. "I'm fine. Just was a little excited and forgot about my leg. I haven't done that in a long time."

He slid his hands under me and set me back on the bed. This was the kind of treatment a girl could get used to.

"You need to be more careful."

"Right? But this is so exciting. You heard everything, didn't you?"

"Yeah, it was sort of hard to miss the way you were screaming."

"I'm sorry."

"No. It's great."

I threw my arms around his neck. "It's because this is the kind of publicity the cafe needs. And even the town. A great restaurant can do amazing things for a town, you know."

"Yes, it can."

"Oh, my God. I need to call Scutt."

"Scutt?"

"Scuttlebutt, my brother. He's the one responsible for this." After I filled Rusty in, I called my little brother.

"Glenn, you won't believe what just happened."

I told him about Mr. Ammons and thanked him. I even promised to buy him a new video game.

"See, I told ya I'd handle it!" Glenn said.

"You rock, dude!"

"Why'd you call me Glenn?"

"Because you are growing up and I think I'm going to have to ditch your nickname. You're a businessman now."

"But I like it when you call me Scuttlebutt. Maybe you can call me Glenn in public."

"Deal. Now I've gotta go, but I'll call you later. Have I told you how much I love you?"

"Yeah. But that's kinda gross, Lilou." I could only imagine the crests of his cheekbones turning bright rosy. He hated when I said things like this. I adored this kid and he was going to know it. One thing I learned in rehab and how I nearly died was our time on this Earth was precious and we needed to make sure the ones we loved knew how much they meant to us.

"Well, get used to hearing it a lot because I'm going to be telling you a lot."

"Hey, why didn't you come home last night?"

Now it was my turn for my cheeks to turn scarlet. "Um, I, er, that's to say, I had some business to do with Jackson." I cringed when I lied. But I could never tell him I spent the night with Rusty.

"Oh, cool. I'll see you around."

When I looked at Rusty, he already knew.

"I'm sorry," he said.

"For what?"

"For making you feel like that."

"It was my choice. I could've gone home. Besides, I'm a grown woman."

"Yeah, but you hated telling that to your brother."

"He's only fourteen, so …"

"I completely understand. But I have to add, last night was the best night of my life."

Smiling, I said, "Mine too."

"So, breakfast?"

"Yes! But let me run home to shower and change. I'll meet you back here as soon as I can."

"Shower with me. I'll so make it worth your while."

"Um, showers are a little tricky for me. You know." I pointed to my leg.

"I'll hold you up the entire time. I'll even wash you. The bathroom has all sorts of hair products."

"Are you sure?"

"You have to ask?" he picked me up and carried me to the massive bathroom.

The shower took much longer than any other shower in my life. Of course, there were some extracurricular activities involved, ones that centered around his dick and me being held up against the wall. I'm pretty damn sure I was going to be deliciously sore for days to come.

When he was drying me off as I sat on the edge of the bed, he asked, "I didn't hurt you, did I?"

"If you had, I would've told you." I pulled him down for a kiss. "You have the most amazing eyes."

"I've always hated them because they're so like my father's."

"Then good thing I never knew him because I have nothing to compare them with other than they're yours and they're gorgeous."

When I was dressed with my hair dried, I left for home

and changed. While I was there, my mom stopped me on my way out of the house.

"Lilou, where were you last night?"

"Mom, what are you doing here?"

"I called out sick."

"Is everything okay?"

"Yeah, just a stomach bug. But where did you spend the night?"

"With Jackson. Um, I've gotta go."

"Lilou, I saw Jackson this morning. I stopped by the cafe to see if you were there. She said she hadn't seen you."

I was a teenager again, getting caught for sneaking out of the house past midnight.

"Okay, Mom. I didn't stay with Jackson. I spent the night with a man I met. His name is Rusty Garrett."

"Oh? Where does he live?"

"In Virginia Beach. I'll have him come over so you can meet him." I quickly tapped his number on my phone and gave him my parents' address. I told him I'd been busted and he had to meet my mom.

"Lilou, I know you're not a teenager anymore, but a text would've been nice. I worried about you all night."

"I'm sorry, Mom. You're right. That was very inconsiderate of me."

It didn't take long for Rusty to get here. When he did, he came to the door and knocked. My mom answered and let him in.

"I think I'm grounded."

"Mrs. Marsten, it was my fault she didn't come home. I take full responsibility, ma'am."

"That's a noble gesture, but my daughter is old enough to take responsibility for her own actions."

"Yes, ma'am, but you see, here's the thing. While this may sound crazy to you and hard to believe, I'm quite positive I'm falling for your daughter. And the only way I know to find out is to spend time with her. The fact she didn't come home was completely my fault because I persuaded her to stay with me. If you're angry with anyone, it should be me. I apologize for any wrongdoing on my part."

"Son, are you willing to make an honest woman out of my daughter?"

"Mom, this isn't the eighteen hundreds," I said. Mom was exasperating.

"I know, sweetheart, but this young man seemed intent on making things right, so I thought I'd see how far he was willing to go."

Rusty said, "The way I feel about her right now, my answer would be yes."

Chapter Sixteen

Rusty

WHAT THE HELL did I just say? Did I just tell Lee's mother that I would marry Lee? Had I lost every ounce of sanity in my brain? Fuck me. I barely knew her.

"Rusty, have you gone mad?" Lee asked.

"I'm not sure." And I wasn't.

Her mom cackled.

"And Mom, aren't you sick?"

"Not really. I was just upset because you hadn't come home all night."

"Jesus. This is crazy here. Rusty, I think we need food because the blood has left your brain and you're saying stupid things."

I held out my hand with one finger extended. "Wait a minute. You know what? I'm not crazy. People fall in love all the time. You told me about your great-grandparents. Why can't we fall fast like that? I'm not saying we have and that we should get married now. *That* is off the charts insane. But I am saying is I believe in us, even though we've just met. And I'm willing to bet that one day, I'm going to be waiting for you at the end of the aisle and you and I will be saying our *I do's*."

Lee waved her hand, saying, "Whatever."

Her mom cackled again, and said, "Lilou, I like this young man. If you know what's good for you, you'll hang on to this one."

"Yeah, okay Mom." Turning to me, Lee said. "Let's go eat."

We got in my truck and I said, "Lilou, huh?"

"Yeah, that's my real name. Lilou Grace Marsten. But most everyone, except my immediate family, calls me Lee."

"Wow."

"What?"

"That's the most beautiful name ever. My foster sister made up her name."

"You mean Midnight, right?"

"Yeah. Her birth name was Velvet. That was her name when she came to live with us and I remember thinking how that name suited her. Her hair is like black velvet. Velvet Summers was her name."

"But that is sort of a crazy name."

"Definitely. Her mom was a drug addict, so you can kind of see where this is going. She was probably high when she named her. But as a kid, I thought it was cool. Not cool now. But your name … totally cool and awesome."

"I've always hated Lilou."

"Why?"

"I don't know. I like Lee better."

Grabbing her hand, I said, "I love it. And sorry I got you in trouble with your mom."

"Don't be. She's happy now after what you said, you crazy fool."

"I may be a lot of things, but a fool isn't one of them. You'll see one day." I smirked at her.

At the cafe, we ordered breakfast from a happy Jackson. She was gloating over the two of us. She laughed when Lee told her how she got into trouble with her mom.

"Just like high school."

"What did you do in high school?" I asked.

"For one, we got into Jackson's grandma's moonshine. We got so trashed it wasn't funny. Then we got in trouble for getting drunk and from her grandma for dipping into her stash."

The thought of the two of them staggering around hammered as hell had me laughing my ass off. "Wish I could've seen that."

Lee held her hand up. "Oh no. It wasn't pretty when we were throwing up all over the place."

"If you can't hold your liquor ..." I shrugged.

"Uh, yeah. We didn't touch that stuff again," I said.

Breakfast was delicious—the best I'd ever eaten. This cafe rivaled any food I'd ever tasted.

"Jackson needs to enter some of those food contests or get on one of the TV shows. Her cooking is amazing," I said.

"I know. She is talented."

We finished eating and Lee informed me she had to work the lunch hour.

"Would it be okay if I just hung out here?"

"What? Are you gonna ogle me all afternoon?"

"Of course. What else would I do in a town like Drummond?"

"You've got a point."

I leaned across the table and pressed my lips to hers.

"If I can help, just let me know. I'm pretty good at chores, you know."

"Can you wash dishes?"

"Pfft. Anyone can do that."

She grabbed my hand and said, "Come on. And bring your dirty dishes with you."

We cleaned up our mess and headed back to the kitchen where Jackson was running the show. There were a couple of helping hands with her, but she had everything under control.

"Hey you two. Tell me about last night," Jackson called out. Her grin was a dead giveaway she knew what we'd been up to.

"I'm not the kiss and tell kind of guy," I called back out.

"Hey Jackson, do you recall an old guy working at Neal's store?" Lee asked.

"Not that I can remember. Why?"

"Rusty was in there yesterday and said there was some old man in there," Lee said.

"Yeah, I went inside to check out that old wooden train set in the window. I was interested in buying it, but he told me it wasn't for sale. Anyway, we had quite a long conversation and then he sent me here to eat."

"I have no idea who that could be. Did you get a name?" Jackson wanted to know.

"Nope. Didn't bother to ask."

Lee was cleaning off the griddle while she spoke. "After lunch, I want to go over there to see if he's still there."

Jackson only shrugged. "Maybe he's an uncle of Neal's or something."

"Maybe. I just think it's kinda weird that neither of us knows him."

"Eh, whatever. I'm glad he sent me a new customer and got you a date."

I laughed as Lee threw a dishcloth at her.

The lunch crowd was thick. I was a quick study at bussing tables and serving drinks. I also helped carry the heavier trays out and later joked around with Lee about sharing her tips.

"You owe me, Lee."

"I do, but not to worry. I'll make this worth it."

I watched her hips sway and it dawned on me how well she walked with her prosthesis. Her slight limp was barely noticeable.

When she was finished for the afternoon, we left the cafe and went down the street to the little woodworking shop. The bell on the door rang when we entered. Neal came and greeted us.

"Hey, Neal. You doing okay?"

"Pretty good, Lee. What about yourself?"

"Good. Neal, this is Rusty. He's visiting from Virginia Beach and was in yesterday."

"No, not yesterday. I was closed. You must've been in the day before. I came down with some stomach thing, so I never opened the shop yesterday."

"Are you sure?" I asked. "I came in and there was an old gentleman in here. I inquired about that train set in the window. He told me it wasn't for sale but sold me some other things. Ducks and fish."

"No. I promise you, there wasn't an old man in here and I didn't open up yesterday."

Lee touched my arm. "Come on, Rusty. You must've been mistaken."

"Yeah, I suppose so."

"See you, Neal," she called out as we left.

When we got outside, I said, "Look, I know you think

I'm nuts, but I swear I saw him. I even have things I bought from that shop. I can show you."

Lee was quiet for a minute as we walked. Then she suddenly stopped and said, "If I show you a picture of someone, could you recognize that man?" she asked.

"I couldn't forget his face if I tried."

"Come on. We're going to my house."

We went back to the cafe and jumped in her car. When we got to her parents' house, she took me inside and dug through some old pictures. She handed me one and asked, "Is this him?"

The picture was aged and worn, but I checked it out closely. "I'm not sure because this man is so much younger. Do you have one of him when he's older?"

"Hang on."

She flipped through another old photo album and continued her search. Finally, she pulled another picture out. "What about this?"

I examined it closely. "Yes! He's still younger but that's him."

Lee smiled. "This is really weird. This is my great-grandfather."

"How in the hell was he in that shop yesterday? This man is dead." I shook the picture in my hand.

"Not only is he dead, but he's also been dead for over thirty years."

Chapter Seventeen

Lee

RUSTY WAS NOT ACCEPTING THIS. His head swiveled as he pointedly gazed at the photo.

This mysterious explanation didn't exactly make much sense to me either. "I think you're right. Don't you see? We didn't meet by coincidence. This guy had everything to do with it. He sent you to me, Rusty. Weird as it may sound, I believe it."

"I felt drawn to you too, but seeing him yesterday puts a whole new brand on the word eerie. I mean, I don't know, Lee. How can that be?"

"I honestly can't say."

"Lee? Rusty? What are you two up to?" It was Mom. She stared at us curiously as we sat among the pile of pictures.

"Mom, you need to sit down and listen to this."

"What is it? Is everything okay?"

I motioned toward the chair, saying, "Yeah, but just sit. We'll explain."

She took a seat and then I launched into my explanation of what happened. "Rusty saw him. Great-Granddad. At Neal's woodworking shop."

Mom took a deep breath. "Lee, honey, I think this is a marvelous story, but—"

"Mom, it's not a story. We went to Neal's shop and he was closed yesterday. How could Rusty have bought those items from him and how would he have been able to have described in intricate detail what that shop looked like inside if he hadn't been in there?"

"You bought some things from him, Rusty?"

"Yes, ma'am. I purchased some wooden ducks and some painted fish. I can show you. They're in my truck back at the inn."

Mom tugged on her ear, something she did when she was thinking hard. "Hmm. This is unusual, to say the least."

"That's why we think Great-Granddad had something to do with us meeting. You know his story about the train depot and how I'm helping Jackson with the cafe. Now I'm thinking it had something to do with that. He wanted Rusty to meet me for some reason."

Rusty grabbed my hand. "I already know the reason."

Mom grinned. "It doesn't really matter how you two met, does it. What matters is you did."

"I guess. But isn't it kind of cool it happened this way?" I asked.

"They do say that our loved ones watch over us from above. Maybe your great-granddad felt a special attachment to you, Lilou since you share a bond with him. And that was his way of doing so."

Rusty piped in. "Whatever the case, I wish I could thank the man because he sure did me a solid."

"He was an exceptional man," Mom said.

"Ma'am, can I ask you. Did he do wood carvings?"

"He did. As a matter of fact, we have a few scattered around the house here." Mom got up to go fetch them. I had forgotten about that, mainly because I'd taken them for granted having seen them every day growing up. When Mom returned, she was carrying two beautifully painted mallards. Rusty's eyes widened when he saw them.

"Those are just like the ones I bought yesterday."

"You're kidding," Mom said.

"Not at all. I fell in love with them because of the fine detail." He asked to hold one and then he pointed a few things out. "See the feathering on the white ring around its neck? And how the paint carries that sheen in certain spots? It's almost like the creature has come to life in your hand."

"I've never thought of it that way, but yes, I suppose it does," Mom said.

"They really are spectacular. As soon as he showed them to me, I knew I had to own them. And the fish are amazing too."

"I'm not familiar with the fish."

"I'll bring them over so you can see."

"Maybe he's working some magic from above then, Lilou."

"He must still be carving wood too," I said. Then I told Mom about Glenn's intervening and how we were going to be interviewed for the cafe.

"I'm happy he's been hard at work doing something," she said.

"Yeah, it may help Jackson with her business overall, not to mention the new name."

"New name?"

"Yeah. He came up with this great idea to change the cafe's name to I'll Be Waiting in honor of Great-Granddad."

"Lilou, that's fantastic."

"We thought so. Where is Glenn?"

"At a friend's house."

"Oh, I wanted Rusty to meet him."

"Why don't the two of you pick him up then? I told him I would get him at five."

When I glanced at Rusty, he was already speaking. "We'd love to. I'd really like to meet him."

"Great. And would you like to join us for dinner tonight, Rusty?"

"Uh, no, Mom. We have other plans," I said. Mom's disappointment was etched on her face. So I hastily added, "But we'll stay until Dad gets home so Rusty can meet him."

"Oh, good." That seemed to appease her some.

"We're going to the library now," I said.

"The library?" Mom was more than a little surprised.

"Yeah, I want to look for old pictures of Great-Granddad at the train depot. I didn't know if maybe the library had any on file."

"I wonder if I do somewhere. What are you going to do with them?"

"We want to frame and hang them in the cafe."

Mom pointed to the ceiling. "Ah, that's a wonderful idea. Let me see what's up in the attic. It might take a while."

"That's fine. In the meantime, we'll still check at the library. Come on, Rusty."

On the way, we stopped at the inn to pick up Rusty's purchases from yesterday. When he showed me, I was totally blown away. "These are so much like the mallards Mom has, aren't they?"

"Yes. And I can't wait to show her the fish."

I burst out laughing.

"What?"

"You. You're like a kid with those fish."

"My fish are awesome."

"Yeah, they are. You're proud of your fish, aren't you?"

"You're making fun of me, aren't you?"

"Never. I would never make fun of a man and his fish."

He poked his tongue against his cheek. "Uh huh. You seem like the type that would. I bet you'd make fun of a lot of things."

"Like what?"

Before I could guess what was coming, I was on his lap and his mouth had taken command of mine. "I'm not going to give you the answer to that." Then he kissed me some more.

"Maybe the library can wait for a little while."

He pushed my hair behind my ear. "Mmm. Did you have something else in mind, Lee?"

"Maybe."

"Such as."

"Why don't we go into your room and maybe you'll find out."

"Are you still going to make fun of my fish."

"Huh uh. I wouldn't dare."

He opened the car door and I slid off his lap and out. Then he followed and we walked hand in hand inside. I didn't care that people noticed us. I didn't care if they knew who I was. I didn't care that it was the middle of the afternoon. The only thing I did care about was that I was with Rusty and he made me feel like the most special person on the earth.

Chapter Eighteen

RUSTY

THERE WERE days back when I was young, and my dad said terrible things to me. He told me I would never amount to anything because I was nothing but a stupid skinny kid, and I believed him. I would lie in bed and think of how I would grow old and lonely because I was worthless ... a zero. When I left home, I didn't care about loneliness or getting old anymore. The only thing I cared about was being away from that awful place. Then I knew my future was in my own hands and I could do whatever I wanted. But I was burdened with thoughts of wondering if I'd be the kind of man my dad was. Would I fly into rages and destroy the people I loved? Or would I end up in a relationship only to cause that person pain? Months of therapy helped me understand I had a choice ... a choice to become the person I wanted to become. Standing here with Lee, I'm reminded of those thoughts. Will I be a good man? Will I break the chains of my upbringing and be the man she can be proud of, or will I allow the bastard that raised me to win? I know the answer when I see her ... the way her eyes shine and sparkle ... the way her hair looks as though it was spun from silk ... the way her smile looks like it was made just for me. And the answer is *never*. Never would I allow him to be right. I will always be the better man. My insides clench with this knowledge, the knowledge that I would protect her without regard for my own life.

It was impossible not to touch her. My muscles bunched as I sought for control. Coming off as some lousy high school kid wasn't my idea of how I wanted this to go. But she was so damn beautiful with the way her eyes dug into mine, and her lips slightly parted, it took much more strength than doing fifty pull-ups to keep my cool.

She stepped toward me and that's when I lost it. I wrapped my hand around her tiny waist and pulled her into me.

"I'm going to try to rein it in, but no promises, Lilou Grace Marston." The words came out ragged and hoarse. Then my mouth was on hers as I unbuttoned her shirt. Tugging the top of her bra down, I freed a nipple so I could pinch and tweak it. Her moans spurred me on, so I dropped my head to encase my lips around the tight and firm peak.

The intake of air told me all I needed to know. I inched her toward the bed, working the button and zipper on her jeans. Moving to the other nipple, I repeated my actions, flicking my tongue against the rock hard bud. She arched against me as I got her to the side of the bed. Pushing her backward with the palm of my hand, her ass landed on the mattress and I pulled her pants down, freeing her of them. Dropping to my knees, I spread her wide and tickled her pussy with my nose. Using my fingers to open her up, I slipped my tongue in deep. She tasted of salted honey and I hummed my pleasure. My dick was rock hard, ready for her, but I needed her to feel the pleasure first.

My fingers replaced my tongue while it zeroed in on her clit. She writhed against me, arching her back.

"Yesss," she hissed as her fingers sunk into my hair.

I hooked my finger and pressed down on her G-spot, still keeping up the tongue action. She was dripping by now, and my dick throbbed, causing my balls to ache with the pressure.

"I'm going to come, Rusty," she told me.

I put my mouth over her clit and sucked.

"Oh, God," she cried as her pussy clamped down on my finger. The little pulsing motions ensued during her orgasm. When they eased, I pulled out and wiped my face on the sheet.

She lifted up her head, saying, "That was epic."

"Glad you liked it, but there's more to come."

"Come. I like that." She laughed.

I stripped, grabbed some condoms, and stepped back to the bed.

"I want to taste you," she said.

"Oh, Lee, I don't know."

Her crinkled brow told me I'd hurt her. "No, it's not what you think. If you wrap that gorgeous mouth of yours around me, I won't last a minute."

"Would that be so bad?"

"No, it would be great. But I want you to feel pleasure too."

"I just did."

"I know but …"

"I want to, Rusty."

When I didn't say anything, she added, "I never thought I'd have to beg you to give you a blow job."

"Christ, when you put it like that."

She flicked her hand. "Come to the edge of the bed." So I sat where she'd indicated. Then she dropped down between my knees.

I tipped her chin up. "Are you comfortable down there?"

"Yeah. I still have my leg on but yeah."

"Okay, but if you're not, you tell me."

"I will."

She swiped her tongue from base to tip and then repeated it, swirling around the head of my cock, concentrating on the most sensitive part. Then she pushed the whole thing into her mouth, all the way to the base, and started sucking me off. Holy fucking blow job. She was damn good. One of her hands pumped my dick while the other grabbed my sack, squeezing it to perfection.

"Uh, yeah," I said.

She had the right amount of pressure with each stroke and it wasn't long before I said, "I'm gonna come. Like right away."

She sank all the way down, sucked hard, and did this thing with her tongue in the slit and then on the tip.

"Oh, fuck, oh, fuck, oh, fuck." That was my new mantra.

I must've shot the biggest wad down her throat, yet she didn't seem to mind at all. She swallowed every last drop, sucking me dry, and then licking me clean.

"Lee, Lee, Lee, what have you done?"

"I just gave you head."

I could only laugh at that. "You're crazy. You know that, don't you?"

"Uh huh."

"Get up here so I can kiss you."

She climbed on the bed and I grabbed and kissed her, pulling her on top of me. "Now I'm worthless for you."

"I can take a raincheck." Then she bolted up, saying, "Crap, what time is it?"

Checking my watch, I said, "Four. Why?"

"That doesn't give us much time for the library. We need to get Glenn at five."

"We'd better get a move on then."

We laughed our way to the library, with me teasing her about how she gave me dead head—in both heads. "My brain and dick are worthless now."

Once in the library, we had to go to the archives where the old newspapers were kept. Everything was on microfiche, so we began with the time her great-grandfather came home, which was December 1944. We didn't begin to see anything until right before we had to leave. There was one article about him on April 5, 1945, and it included a small photo of him in his army uniform.

"Rusty, we have to leave."

"At least we know where to start when we come back."

"And maybe Mom will find some pictures too."

Since we'd taken my truck, Lee directed me to her brother's friend's house. We both went to the door to get him. He opened the door and eyed me, then his gaze bounced to Lee.

"Glenn, this is my friend Rusty."

I held my hand out for him to shake, which he did. He was a lanky kid of about Lee's height with darker hair than hers, but his eyes were the same shape and color. "Pleased to meet you, Glenn. I've heard all sorts of cool things about you from your sister."

"You have?"

"Well yeah."

"Like what?"

"Like you're a marketing genius and you're going to change the dynamics of the cafe."

He preened. "Oh, that. It was nothing."

"No, that was ingenious and will really help out Jackson. You should be proud of that."

"Okay. How come I've never seen you before?" he asked.

"Good question. That's because I live in Virginia Beach."

"Cool. What do you do over there?"

"I'm in the Navy."

"The Navy?"

"Ever heard of it?" I asked. Lee was biting down on her lip trying not to laugh. By this time we'd gotten to my truck.

"Yeah. I've heard of it. Cool truck. Is it yours?"

"Yeah. Glad you approve."

After we all climbed in and buckled up, Glenn continued his interrogation. "So what do you do in the Navy? Are you on a submarine?" His eyes grew to the size of golf balls.

"Nah. I have a boring job."

"Like what."

"I'm a Navy Seal."

His mouth silently formed the words. "You mean you're one of those guys that goes in somewhere in the middle of the night and kills people?"

"Not exactly, but we do go into places in the middle of the night sometimes."

"Do you kill people?"

Jeez, he was relentless.

"Uh, Glenn, I think you might be asking questions Rusty isn't allowed to answer."

Glenn nodded. "I get it. Top secret stuff and all that."

"Yep. If I tell you, then I'd have to kill you."

Swear to God, the kid's eyes nearly popped out of his head. "No kidding?"

"Nah, I'm just pulling your leg. I'd never tell you so there wouldn't be an issue of me killing you."

"Got it."

Lee gave me the final directive and we pulled into her parents' driveway.

"You staying to eat dinner with us?" Glenn asked.

"Not tonight, Scutt," Lee said.

"I thought you weren't gonna call me that anymore."

"Old habits, you know."

"Why can't you stay?"

"We're staying long enough for Rusty to meet Dad."

"Oh, okay. But you should stay for dinner too."

"We have plans."

"What kind of plans? Kissy face plans?" He puckered up his lips and kissed the air. It was impossible not to chuckle.

Lee swatted at him. "Maybe," she said. "Actually, nosy head, Jackson and I are going to talk about the interview tomorrow."

He put his hand on top of her head. "You have my blessing, young grasshopper."

"Get out of here you little goober."

He bolted away and I said, "That kid has personality."

"And is a pain in the neck."

"You love it."

"I admit it. Come on. Let's meet Dad." She took my hand and led me into the kitchen. Her parents were chatting when we interrupted them

"Dad, I want you to meet Rusty Garrett. Rusty, this is my dad."

"Mr. Marston, a pleasure, sir."

"My wife has been singing your praises. It's glad I am to meet you. She's a handful, that one," he said, lifting his thumb in the direction of Lee.

"Dad! I'm not that bad."

"Sure you're not. Have I got some stories for you," he said.

"I was in high school then. Jeez, can a girl catch a break?"

"Lee, you know better than to ask that." He laughed.

"I'd be interested in hearing all about those stories, sir," I said.

We hung out for a while and then headed out to meet Jackson. On the way to the car, I asked, "Are we really meeting Jackson, or did you just make that up?"

"We really are, and I don't lie, Rusty."

"Good, because I confess, that worried me a little."

Lee and Jackson talked about what they wanted to cover and how they'd squeeze it into the interview if Mr. Ammons didn't directly ask them the right questions. Jackson left, and we went to grab some dinner. We decided to get a pizza and eat it in the room.

We were stretched out on the sofa, eating and watching TV when Lee asked me what day I was going home.

"I have to leave the day after tomorrow, but let's not think about it."

"Good idea. That's too soon."

There'd been something I'd wanted to mention to her. I set my paper plate on the coffee table and leaned forward. Then I took her hand and said, "I've been thinking. Why don't you come back to Virginia Beach with me?

Chapter Nineteen

LEE

GO BACK to Virginia Beach with him? Wasn't that moving a bit too fast? Make that way too fast.

"Wait. I think you got the wrong impression. I meant just for a few days or so."

Now I felt relieved but also like the biggest dork for jumping to such an extreme conclusion. "Riiiggghhht. I knew that. Yes. Just a few days. That would be totally cool."

"You didn't think I meant ... no, you wouldn't have ... would you?"

"No," I said, waving my hand through the air. But I had. I definitely had. And for that brief moment, I panicked but did wonder what it would be like to be with Rusty. Would we mesh? Would we work? No doubt there is something major between us, something tethering us together. I really don't want to think about him leaving. And I want to explore *us*. "I'd love to go back with you. But

I need to clear it with Jackson since I've committed to her in a way."

"Sure, I understand. I'd really love to show you around where I live, introduce you to all the guys, give you a tour of ... am I moving too fast? Just tell me if I am."

"I don't think you can take me to work, Rusty. I don't have top security clearance."

"Right. But you can meet my squadron. There are a few jerkoffs in there, but for the most part, they're top notch guys."

"You say jerkoffs with affection, as if you like that about them."

"I do. It's what makes them who they are. You've met those people who seem to be assholes, but really aren't? That's what I'm talking about."

"I know what you mean. They're the ones who go on and on and can always one up you but will have your back in a heartbeat."

"Exactly. Hey, will you get in trouble if you spend the night with me?" he asks.

"I'm pretty sure I'm past the getting grounded age."

"Yeah, but Lee, I want your parents to like and trust me. I don't want them to think I'm taking advantage of their daughter."

"Don't worry about what my parents think. I'll handle them."

He pulled me on top of his lap. "And will you handle me too?"

"You bet I will."

I was pretty sure he was going to be doing most of the handling, but I wouldn't tell him that. When his lips landed on mine, I sighed because he had a way of making me forget everything but him. All I wanted was Rusty. But I didn't want to think about our time together coming to a rapid end.

THE NEXT MORNING, Rusty drove with me to the cafe. He was going to help with work so we could get finished to talk with Mr. Ammons, who was coming to the cafe for the interview. It seemed the breakfast and lunch crowds were thicker than usual. We worked our tails off, sliding from breakfast straight into lunch.

Rusty was a big help in keeping tables cleared and dishes washed. Every time there was an order ready, he didn't hesitate to deliver it.

"I'm going to miss his help when he leaves," Jackson commented.

"Me too," I agreed.

"You're going to miss him for other things, Lee." She snickered.

"Oh shut up. By the way, would you mind me being gone a few days?"

"Hell yes, I'll mind, but I won't ever stop you. What's up?"

"Rusty wants me to go back to Virginia Beach with him for a few days."

"Oh my freakin' God. That's awesome!"

"Yeah."

"Wipe that dreamy look off your face before you screw up an order, girl."

Laughing, I said, "I don't have a dreamy look on my face."

"Like hell you don't."

Rusty came through the swinging doors and we both clamped our mouths shut. "You two talking about me?"

"Nope. We were talking about me," I said. Then one of Jackson's assistants dropped a pan. I flinched, and then hit the ground. Rusty was by my side in an instant.

"You okay?" he asked.

"Yeah." I let out a shaky laugh. "Just a little residual PTSD. You know, loud noises." Rusty helped me to my feet.

"You sure you're okay?" he asked again.

"Yes."

He nudged my shoulder. "Well, you two must've been talking about me before that happened."

"Why do you say that?"

"It was sure quiet when I walked in. Usually you two are babbling up a storm."

Neither Jackson nor I said a word. He chuckled and walked out with a tray of food to be delivered.

"He's a good guy, Lee."

"Yeah, he is. I think."

"What's that supposed to mean?"

"What if he's some serial killer?"

"Oh for the love of God. Do you honestly think that?"

"I don't know."

Jackson scratched her head. "Google him. If he is, it'll come up."

"Yeah. True."

"Google his name and the navy and see what you get."

"Okay."

"Lee, if you don't do it I will."

"I'll do it but not this minute."

The door swung open again and Rusty said, "If you give me a minute, I'll google my own self and show you both what comes up. But I can show you all my credentials if you'd like. I am not opposed to that at all."

I'd never been so embarrassed in all my life. I covered my face and bowed my head.

He set the tray he was carrying down and came to my side. "Lee, it's fine. If there's one thing I want, it's for you to feel safe around me."

"You'd think I would've thought of that before I'd spent the night with you."

"There is that," he said with a grin. Then he hugged me into his side.

"Hey you two, we don't have time for chit-chat," Jackson yelled, then winked.

"Right," I said, getting back to my work. I went out to check on the customers and the day rushed by. After our last guest was served their food, I noticed a middle-aged man enter the cafe. I went to the hostess stand to greet him.

"Are you Mr. Ammons by any chance?"

"I am."

I held out my hand saying, "I'm Lee Marston. Welcome to the new I'll Be Waiting Cafe. Let me get you seated and let Jackson know you're here."

I got him settled and took his drink order, then went back to the kitchen.

"He's here, Jackson."

"Great. She finished up cleaning the griddle, and washed her hands, then took off her chef's coat.

"Rusty, do you mind handling our last customer?"

"Not at all. The only thing is, I don't know how to handle the register."

"Just grab us when they're ready," I said.

We went to join Mr. Ammons.

He fired off questions about my great-grandfather and his connection to the cafe. Jackson and I filled him in on all the details, leaving nothing out. We watched as he scribbled down note after note and when I got to the part about how we shared similar war injuries, he dropped his pen and exclaimed, "This is incredible. How has this story not been picked up by anyone?"

Shrugging, I said, "I don't know. But I'm drawn to this place and imagine my surprise when I found one of my best friends from high school was the owner."

Then Jackson grabbed my hand. "Aren't you going to tell him about Rusty?"

Mr. Ammons asked, "Who's Rusty?"

"I'm Rusty," he answered, placing a refill of tea in front of Mr. Ammons.

"And how do you fit into all this?" Mr. Ammons asked.

I went on to fill him in on that part of the story, leaving out the weird part of Rusty meeting my maybe Great-Granddad in the wood shop. That was just way too freaky to share with anyone.

"Wow. Was this love at first sight?"

Oh, God. I didn't expect that from him.

Rusty only smiled and I did too. "I think we'll reserve that answer for now," I said.

"I think I have enough for a great story that the people in these parts will absolutely adore."

"Mr. Ammons, do you think the newspaper would have any archived photos from back in 1944. I know my great-granddad was here every day so I'm pretty sure someone had to have come around and taken some. We'd love to have some copies to hang on the walls here."

"Let me see what I can do for you."

After he was gone, we were sure I'll Be Waiting would get a huge surge in business.

"Lee, if you're going back to Virginia Beach with Rusty, you'd better go tomorrow after the photo shoot. I have a feeling I'm going to need some extra hands around here after that article runs."

Mr. Ammons was sending a photographer from the newspaper to take photos of the cafe during breakfast tomorrow. And Jackson was right. This could have the potential to explode her business.

Chapter Twenty

RUSTY

WE ARRIVED at the cafe by six, even though they didn't open until seven. Jackson was already busy, getting things going for her pancake batter and other specialties she served.

"I ought to stay in the kitchen for those pictures, ladies."

"No way," Lee said. "We've already been through this." And we had. She was insistent I join in. It wasn't all her though. Mr. Ammons requested I come along because of our story that Lee shared.

"It's sort of awkward. I mean, this is Jackson's time to shine and I don't really belong."

"Rusty, it's not like you're going to steal the show or anything. You're only going to add to it."

There was no point in arguing any further, so I went about the cafe setting things up. The photographer was set to arrive around eight.

We opened the doors at seven and tables began filling up. At eight, a young guy entered with a couple of cameras slung around his neck and Lee greeted him. He introduced himself as Greg and didn't wait to start snapping away. The only posed shots he took were of Lee and Jackson holding up platters of some of the food they served for breakfast. The guy must've taken hundreds of photos and when he was done, I made him sit and eat. I recommended the house specialty—pancakes—and he didn't leave a crumb on his plate. He promised to email Jackson a link to all the pictures.

"I think you two have hit the jackpot," I said.

Lee brushed a lock a hair out of her eyes and said, "Yeah. I agree. That guy took pictures of everything. He wanted to see the menu too and asked about our hours of operation. Mr. Ammons said he'd put that in the article, but I pointed them out on the menu and Greg snapped a few shots of them."

"Have you ever heard of a restaurant in Virginia Beach called She Sells Seafood?" I asked.

Jackson looked up from her prep station. "Who hasn't. That place is known all over the state."

"From what I understand, it takes weeks to get a reservation, and it was opened by a young woman who wanted to make a name for herself. She started out small and grew into what it is today by serving great food and pretty much word of mouth. With the help of that newspaper business, that could be you in a few years."

"Yeah, all except for one glaring detail," Jackson said.

"What's that?" I asked her.

"Drummond is nothing but a tiny blip on the radar compared to Virginia Beach, which is a huge tourist area."

"True, but with that comes a ton of competition. You

have none here. Zero. But what you do have is opportunity."

"Rusty has a point, Jackson."

"Just you two keep your fingers crossed and I'm going to take it one day at a time."

"Hey, did you put that order in for the new sign yet?" Lee asked.

"Yeah, and they're coming up with some designs for me to look at. They said they'd have something in the next couple of days."

Lee clapped her hands. "Promise you'll email them so I can see."

"Of course. Which reminds me, you guys should get out of here."

"But what about lunch?" Lee asked.

"We were planning on leaving after that," I said.

"Don't be ridiculous. I can handle that. You guys go and Lee, I'll see you in a few days."

Lee grabbed my hand and off we went. We had to stop at her place in order for her to pack a bag, and then she followed me back to Virginia Beach. The drive was right under an hour, and we talked on our phones the entire trip since she followed behind me in her car. She told me I was a manly man driving my big truck. I told her my big truck didn't make me manly. It was the beast in my pants that did it.

"I'm shocked and hurt you've already forgotten about him."

"I didn't say I'd forgotten about him. How could I? He visited me last night."

"Maybe we need to pull over so he can visit you again." The mere thought had the beast getting hard.

"Haha. Is your beast getting anxious?"

"He's not my beast, he's yours. When you're not around, he's nothing but a harmless pussycat."

I heard her giggling into the phone. "I can't believe you admitted that."

"Hey, honest and tell it like it is."

"Yeah, but not that."

"I'm comfortable in my manhood." And I was. "It took years of therapy but I'm there now."

"Will you ever give me the details?" she asked.

"You already know the basics."

"But I want to know everything."

"No, you don't. It's an ugly messy story that I don't want to taint your beautiful mind with."

"I have scars, too, you know."

"Yes, but yours are from an act of heroism, not from a sadistic father."

Her voice softened. "I wish I was sitting next to you right now."

"I always wish you were sitting next to me."

We arrived at my apartment and I carried our bags inside. My place was small—a one bedroom, which suited me fine. I hoped she didn't think it was lame.

"The bedroom is back there, along with the bathroom."

"This is really nice," she said. "You're so organized."

"Military life teaches you to be."

"I liked that part of it."

"Same here. I was thinking. I don't have anything in here as far as food goes. How about we do a store run and then we can decide if we want to eat in or go out."

"I know exactly what I want to do," she said.

"Oh?"

"I want to eat Rusty's Rockin' Ribs."

"Right. You are going to make me work, aren't you?"

"Yep. And then I want to feel the beast."

"You do, huh?"

She nodded, and her eyes went straight to my crotch. That wasn't good. "I have a feeling the beast will be unleashed before you are served those Rockin' Ribs, as you're calling them."

"If that's the case, we'd better get a move on and we also better get some snack foods so I can keep up my strength."

"Sure thing. I don't want my woman to get weak from hunger."

At the grocery store, we stocked up on snacks, beverages, and I even bought a couple bottles of wine for Lee. She mentioned she liked it, so I figured I might impress her. I wasn't much of a drinker, only a few beers here and there, all on account of my parents. But that wasn't any reason for her not to enjoy a nice glass of the Chardonnay she'd mentioned she'd liked.

I had to get a move on to get the ribs going since they had to cook for a few hours. I went to work on them and she took care of the other stuff.

Once the ribs were going, I had the idea that we could get a little bedroom time. As we were kissing, my phone went off.

"Do you need to get that?" she asked.

"No, ignore it." And we went back to kissing. I was about to remove her top when the phone went off again. I pushed it away and continued to take her shirt off. But this time, the phone didn't stop. As soon as it went to my voicemail, it would start ringing again.

"Dammit, something must be up. I'm gonna have to take this."

"It's fine."

"Garrett."

"Garrett, Thompson here. I hate to do this to you, man. But I need you to report in. I know your leave isn't up for three more days, but I'm short two men. We have two down with some stomach bug and they can't travel for three days. Doctor's orders. I need you in first thing in the morning. Wheels are up at eight."

"No way."

"I know, and I wouldn't call you unless it was an emergency. We're not on secure lines so I can't let you know the circumstances. But just be here at seven sharp."

"Yes, sir. How long?"

"Four, five at the most."

"Right. See you at seven."

"Thanks, Garrett."

"Dammit. I should've known better than to answer that."

"What?"

I have to report in at seven. I'm going on a mission and have to be gone four or five days."

"Oh, no."

"Will you promise me something?"

"Anything."

"Will you be here for me when I get back?"

She wrapped her arms around me and pulled me close. "You go and do your duty, and know that while you're gone, I'll be waiting. Always."

I touched my lips to her warm plump ones and my heart was at peace, knowing she'd be here for me ... waiting, just like her great-granddad had done all those years ago.

Chapter Twenty-One

LEE

"WHAT ARE YOU DOING BACK HERE?" Jackson asked. As soon as I explained, her arms were hugging me.

"I'm so worried. Those aren't your everyday missions they go on."

"What do you mean?"

"He's a Seal, remember?" I reminded her.

"Shit. I wasn't thinking. But Seals have stellar skills, right? I mean they're trained to be the best of the best, right?" she asked.

"Sure."

"Then he's golden." She held her hands out.

"Okay, wow ... he's got nothing to worry about like no IED's or anything at all."

"Double shit. I'm sorry."

"No, it's okay, you're only trying to help."

"Don't they give them super special equipment and stuff?"

"I don't really know what they give them. All I know is they are heads above any other soldier. They practically torture the dudes in training and most don't make it a quarter of the way through. You have to have balls of steel to become a Seal."

Jackson grabbed my hands. "See. He'll be fine. And this isn't his first rodeo."

I gave hers a squeeze and said, "I hope you're right. I really do."

"Lee, if it were you on that mission, what would you want Rusty to do?"

"I'd want him to live his life, and not worry excessively about me."

"Exactly."

I pondered my situation for a second, then said, "Well then, put me to work so I can get my mind off this."

She saluted me and said, "Yes, sir."

"That would be ma'am."

She fake punched my shoulder and gave me a dose of chores to do. Then when I finished, she called me over to her laptop.

"Which is your favorite?"

She was looking at a series of new signs for the shop.

"Ooh, I love this one." I pointed to the one on the bottom. It had a train faded in the background and in contemporary script was written in black *I'll Be Waiting.* Centered beneath it in smaller but old-fashioned font in black too was *The Depot Cafe*. "This one is so cool. It represents everything. What do you think?"

"That was my favorite too. I was hoping it was yours."

"Are you going to place the order?"

"You know it. I want it up as soon as possible."

"Did they give you a timeframe?"

"They said they could have it ready in less than a week."

I was every bit as excited as Jackson about this.

"Any word about the article?" I asked.

Jackson snapped her fingers. "Mr. Ammons called and said he would run it whenever we wanted. We need to have it coincide with the new name of the café."

"Yes. Maybe you should give him a call and let him know."

"I will. He also said he found some old pictures of your great-grandfather. He's bringing them over tomorrow with a few copies of the paper."

My eyes practically bugged out. "You're kidding."

"I'm not. He was really happy about them too."

"I wasn't sure …" I stared off into the distance, but then I said, "I have to call Glenn. He needs to hear this." When I did, he was yelling so loud I held the phone away from my ear and even Jackson heard him.

She hollered out, "Dude, you the man!"

"Dang right I am," he shouted back.

I ended the call and told her he was going to be talking himself up something big. "Mom and Dad will have their hands full with him."

"He's a great kid though. Nothing like us."

"He hasn't hit that age yet. Just wait."

That night, as I tried to sleep, I thought about where in the world Rusty might be. Electricity crawled across my nerves as worry fired them to life. I never got a chance to ask him about when we could communicate. Everything about this trip was so sudden, it made me question whether or not I was ready for this type of a relationship. Even though I had been a marine and was familiar with that life, there were stark differences between what I had done and what he was doing. The danger he faced was on a much greater level than I ever had. But then I thought about how my great-granddad left for the war to fight for our freedom only to return home to an empty house. I wouldn't let that happen to Rusty. He went on these missions to save people at a great cost to himself. I would certainly wait for him. My heart cracked every time I thought of the pain he endured as a child growing up in that loveless home. My family was loving and caring, and my mind couldn't wrap itself around the horrors he had faced. How proud his parents should've been of him, instead of beating and mentally abusing him.

Piecing together what little bit I knew of his past, I made a hasty decision. My laptop was across the room on the desk, so I hopped over to it and got back in bed. At first, I felt like I was invading Rusty's privacy and maybe I was. He did tell me to google him. I never did. And I had this pressing need to know more about him, to find out what I could. So without any further hesitation, I typed in his full name, Ruston James Garret.

I hadn't expected the page to fill up with entry after entry of nothing but information on the man, Ruston Garrett, the criminal. I had no idea that Rusty was named after his father. What a terrible reminder to have that moniker.

When I began reading, I was stunned. The charges against this man were terrible, but then when I saw Midnight Drake's name linked, I clicked over and read all the articles about her. That's when I first saw Rusty's name and his testimony against his father.

I stopped reading so many times because my eyes were blurred with tears. What Midnight endured was beyond comprehension. My heart and gut ached for her. I wasn't sure how she made it through that carnage of a life to become who she is today. From all accounts, she was an amazing survivor.

And Rusty ... my god, reading about how he felt responsible for what was happening to her when he was only a young boy. The emotions that played out in the courtroom must've been off the charts. How I wish I had been there to help him. My heart was almost punching through my ribcage as it beat like mad.

Oh, Rusty. I wish I could've been there to help you get through all that.

And then my brain bounced to how it must've been for him growing up in a house without any affection from his mom. He said she was drunk all the time, most likely trying to avoid his dad. He never was shown any love at all. How did he manage? And more to the point, how did he end up normal?

He'd talked about the therapy he'd gone through. I wondered if he still goes. Shame washed over me briefly. I remembered my therapy sessions with my shrink and how I thought I didn't need them ... that I was stronger than that. Rusty was probably much bigger of a person than I and realized in order to deal with the emotional upheaval of his youth, he'd need the help. I was too hard-headed at first.

By the time I closed my laptop, it was after two in the morning. Six thirty would be here all too soon. I was going to be worthless the next day. But as I was falling asleep, I vowed to be the best girl Rusty had ever known and that I would show him love like he'd never seen it. Love. Where the hell did that come from?

Chapter Twenty-Two

RUSTY

"FUCK. How the hell did we find ourselves in another FUBAR?" Wilson yelled.

"No idea. Just keep going." I yelled back. This was supposed to be another fast mover. We'd been dropped in at darkness from a bird in the middle of Iran. Not my favorite place. Too much shit happening here for my tastes. We were supposed to pull out one man—a very important man who had very important information. But that target had too many other people who wanted him as much as we did. That's how we found ourselves in the crossfire between the Irani's and the rest of the motherfucking world—or so it seemed.

Now we were hoofing it to our supposed pick up point. Only that hadn't worked out quite like we'd planned. Our bird took a damn hit and we lost her. No survivors either. We ran to the crash and rigged it with C4 just to make sure the enemy couldn't retrieve any vital information from the craft. Then we were off again. The looming question was —to where?

"Any ideas of our final destination?" Wilson asked.

"Waiting to hear," Thompson replied. I did know one thing. We needed the fuck out of this country. We'd dropped outside of a small town called Darkhovin, which was the site of a nuclear facility. Our contact was supposed to provide us vital information regarding that site and its role in Iran's nuclear arms program. Then shit went south.

"We need to get to Basra, or over the border at the very least. We're not that far. Iraq is what? Seventy kilos?" I asked.

"About a hundred, give or take," Shelton, another one of our group answered.

"We're headed that way. At least we don't have any damn mountains to navigate," Thompson said.

And wasn't that the truth. Our asset wasn't exactly in prime physical condition. He was elderly and didn't appear to be up to a one hundred kilo jaunt by any means. We'd be piggybacking him by the end of the night if I were a guessing guy.

"But the bad part is we don't have much cover either. We're gonna need some means of transportation if we're to do this," someone said.

"Oh, you don't think we can escape an entire regiment of Irani police?" I asked, sarcasm coating my words.

"I'm going to disregard that comment, Garrett," Thompson said.

"Yes, sir." We were good and truly fucked if we didn't come up with something and fast. Then the little old guy we'd come to heist spoke up.

"Excuse me. I can help."

"What did you say?" Thompson was the one who asked but all of us whipped around to stare at him. He was a small guy, short in stature and there wasn't much to him in the form of muscle. A good strong wind could knock him on his tiny ass.

"I said, I help you find vehicle. For you to escape."

"Where? The vehicle," Wilson prodded.

An arm, not much larger than an adolescent's, pointed to a building across the road. "There." He wore the traditional dishdasha, or long tunic, with loose fitting trousers underneath, and his head bore a keffiyeh held in place by an agal. The dishdasha was old and worn so it was easy to see his arms through it.

"It has to be large enough to fit all of us," Thompson told him.

"Yes. Is large. A ... uh, what you call. Truck."

Thompson edged his way closer to the man. "And this truck runs okay?"

"Yes. Is good."

Using two fingers, Thompson pointed to two men. "You two, go now. Check it out. If it's good, we're dust in the wind."

"Copy that, Captain."

We waited in silence, almost afraid to say or think anything, until Thompson's radio crackled to life. "Rover to base. We have a live wire. On the move. Over."

"Copy that Rover. Herd will be ready for the cattle drive. Over."

"Copy that base. Meet you at the trough."

There was an unused fountain in the back of the building we were holed up in, so we filed toward it, waiting for our wheels to show up. When they did, we would've laughed if they weren't our ticket to paradise. The best way to describe it was a rust bucket with an active engine in it. The front bumper dangled by a thread, but by God, we all fit.

"Go, go," one of the men yelled as soon as we were all on board. I was the navigator, as usual, and plotted our course to freedom. Basra was only about ten miles on the other side of the border so if we could make it that far, we could always ditch the jalopy and walk the rest of the way.

"Wilson, how much fuel do we have?"

"No clue. There isn't a gas gauge."

"What?"

"Look."

The gas gauge was busted out. "Damn. This is a new one on me." I turned to the rear and hollered, "Hey, Amir, how much petrol does this have?"

"Good petrol," Amir answered.

Wilson shrugged. "Guess that means we're okay."

"I sure hope so."

But we were far from being in the clear. Even though the helicopter explosion had diverted the attention away from us, and we had escaped without being noticed, there were still checkpoints we had to avoid.

Hitting my comm link, I asked, "Eagle 1, we are in the wind. Request a clear path to freedom. Over."

"Copy that Rover. Calculating."

Waiting for my answer, I checked out our surroundings and my GPS. Wilson was headed in the right direction. My radio hissed. "Rover, continue bearing west. In a quarter mile, you will detour to the left for one-tenth of a mile. Then return to course. Over."

"Copy that Eagle 1. Over." I calculated the route and saw our turn. "Okay Wilson, you're coming up to the turn, and this will be a shorty. Then you're turning again."

"Got it."

He stuck with my directions and I jumped back on the radio. "Eagle 1, this is Rover waiting for our next directive. Over."

"Rover, you are clear for one mile. Over."

"Copy that. Over."

"Stay the course for a mile," I told Wilson.

The radio sputtered again. "Rover, in a half a mile, you will head north for a half mile and then you'll go west again. Over."

"Copy that. Over."

"You got that Wilson?" I asked.

"Copy that."

We zigzagged our way out of the area until we were in no man's land and then we had radio silence for about forty minutes. When it came to life again, our directions were clear. "Rover, abandon wheels and continue on foot. The road to freedom is closed until tomorrow. All other options are blocked. Trek two point three miles on westerly route to safety and wait for oh dark thirty for freedom. Over."

"Copy that. Over." The rest of it would be made on foot.

We ended up spending the night and day in an abandoned structure that was what we called an Irani farmhouse. There were old animal pens outside and water troughs. It was hot, and we tried to catch some shuteye.

We had enough food and water to share so we were fine on those accounts. This was when patience ruled. I drew on my background and how I'd been raised. Everyone else had been raised in a cushy home, comparatively speaking. This was where I was one step ahead of them. I sank into my reserves and thought about how Midnight had survived all those nights. How she did it alone, I don't know, but I remembered praying for her as a kid, hoping he'd stop raping her and beating me. Tonight was a different story. Even though the stakes were larger and we were playing for our lives, in my soul I knew all would be well. No matter what happened, life would never be that bad again. I would die first.

When darkness fell, we waited until after midnight to make our move. We reached the crossing at the right time, the right place, but we didn't anticipate the wrong company being there, waiting for us. We don't know how or why but it didn't matter. We needed to get through and protect our asset.

Fortunately for everyone, even though a lot of gunfire was exchanged, they made it through unscathed. Unfortunately for me, I didn't. I took a shot to the upper chest and one to the thigh. Luckily my Kevlar saved my life on the chest shot and the one to the leg missed my femoral artery. I made it across, but they had to drag my ass the rest of the way. I blacked out on evac.

Chapter Twenty-Three

L<small>EE</small>

FIVE DAYS PASSED and no news from Rusty. Then it was a week. Now I was at day ten and my gut was telling me something went terribly wrong. Not really knowing what to expect, each day grew worse. We'd parted so quickly, I hadn't thought to ask him if and when he'd call. My tattered nerves couldn't have been more frayed. The noose of panic threatened to squeeze the air from my lungs, but I drove it away and kept on going.

"I screwed up another order, Jackson."

Her breath wheezed past her lips. "Don't worry about it. Did you find who it belonged to?"

"Yeah, but it's cold. Can you fix up another batch of banana pancakes and an omelet of the day?"

"On it." She went at it and then said, "Lee, I think you need to head over to Virginia Beach and wait there for him."

"Oh, I don't know."

"I do." Her voice was firm. "You know that's the first place he's going to go. And you did say he gave you a key."

"Yeah, but, what will I do while I'm there?"

"Explore. It's a super cool town and you know it. You've been there plenty of times."

"Sure, but … I just don't know."

She slid the pancake order up to me along with the omelet.

"That was fast," I said.

"You know I have some sitting on the side."

"Oh, yeah."

"See, this is what I mean. Your head isn't on straight right now. You don't need to be here. After breakfast is over, go home, pack a bag, and leave."

"Maybe you're right."

"Lee, I know I'm right. How long has it been?"

"Eleven days."

"Do it."

After the breakfast rush ended, I drove home to pack. I wasn't sure how long I'd be gone so it wasn't easy deciding what to take. I threw in everything but the kitchen sink. My large bag was bursting at the seams and Glenn helped me drag it out to the car.

"How long will you be gone, Lilou?"

"I don't know, Scutt. I have to see what's going on with Rusty."

"You really like that guy, don't you?"

"Yeah, I sort of do."

"It's cool. He's okay by me. I like him."

"You do?"

"Yeah. His truck is cool, and he didn't treat me like I was annoying."

"No, he didn't, did he?"

"Huh uh. I'm gonna miss you."

"I'll miss you too, but it's not like I'm going forever or anything."

"I know, but I kinda got used to having you around."

"True. Same here. You're my favorite brother."

"Lilou, I'm your only brother. Don't act like such a loser." Then he held out his fist for me to bump.

"To hell with that." I pulled him in for a hug.

"Jeez. Don't get all gooey on me. You know I hate that." He shuddered, and I chuckled.

"Sure. It's why I do it. Love you, dude. Tell Mom and Dad I'll call."

He stood there as I drove away. The car ate up the miles between Drummond and Virginia Beach and in less than an hour, I was pulling into Rusty's parking lot.

A sense of doom settled over me as I unlocked his door. I dragged my large duffle into his apartment, and not without great difficulty either. Once I got into his bedroom, I sat on his bed and grabbed his pillow. I still smelled his scent as I pressed it to my nose.

Dear God, please let him be safe.

I hope my little prayer was not only heard but answered too. I knew there wouldn't be any salvageable food in the refrigerator, so I emptied it out and dumped the trash in the dumpster. Then I went to the store to stock up.

The next two days I did as Jackson suggested—I explored the beachside town. On the third morning, I was sipping coffee and watching TV, when I heard a key in the lock. My excitement surged and I knocked my cup over, drenching my shirt in the process. Before I could reach the door to greet Rusty, it was opened by not Rusty, but two strangers.

"Who are you?" I asked.

"Uh, I think we should be asking you that question," one of them answered.

"I'm Lee Marston, Rusty's girlfriend."

They looked at each other and one said, "Now it all makes sense."

"What makes sense?" I asked.

"Lee, can you sit down?"

"What's wrong? Where's Rusty? I haven't heard from him in two weeks."

"Please sit and we'll explain everything."

I dabbed at my soaked shirt and plopped back on the sofa. "Is he okay?"

"First, I'm Stephen Wilson and this is Eric Shelton. We're in the same squadron with Garrett. I'm not sure how much you know ..." his voice trailed off.

"He's a Seal and he went out on a mission two weeks ago."

"Right. So while we were out, things got a little messed up and Garrett got shot."

I pushed to my feet, hands in the air. "Wait. What? He got shot? Is he okay? Where is he?" My heart was jumping out of my chest and I was pretty sure it was bouncing across the living room floor by now.

"Calm down, he's fine."

"Please, Lee, can you sit?" I'm not even sure which one of them spoke. All I could picture was Rusty lying somewhere bleeding out.

"Sit? How can I sit when he could be dying?" Were they crazy?

"He's not dying. He took a hit to the chest, but his Kevlar handled that. The other one hit his thigh. It missed his artery and he's fine. It passed through, nicked the bone though, so he's pretty damn sore. But that's it. He'll make a full recovery with no after effects," Wilson said.

My butt hit the sofa again as I processed everything.

His Kevlar took the hit, but he could've died. Oh God! "His leg is okay though? Nothing permanent?"

"Nothing permanent. He'll be off the active duty list until he's fully recovered though. Maybe eight to twelve weeks." Wilson started laughing. "You're gonna have your hands full."

I gave him an odd look. "Why do you say that?" And how could he even laugh at a time like this?

"Keeping that man still for the next couple of weeks … you'll figure it out," Shelton said.

Then I asked, "Where is he now and why didn't he call?" Panic still edged my tone.

"Lee, he's fine. Seriously. He's still at Ramstein," Shelton said.

"Oh, I know that place well."

"How do you know Ramstein."

"Ex-jarhead here." Then I lifted up my leg. "IED."

"No shit." Shelton whistled. "Thank you for your service, ma'am." And both of them stood and saluted me.

"Sit your asses back down. Why didn't he call me?"

"That I can't answer," Wilson said. "But it may be because we don't carry our regular cell phones with us when we go and he may not have remembered your number. But I don't know for sure."

That probably was it. "Can you get me in touch with him now?"

"I think so. Let me try," Wilson said.

"Wait. Why did you come here if he's not home?" I asked.

"Oh. He is coming home. Tomorrow. He'll be transferred to Walter Reed and then released," Wilson said. "We stopped by to pick up some things for him."

"Don't call him. I want to surprise him. What does he need? I can take it."

"You know Walter Reed?" Shelton asked.

"I was there for months."

"Right. Stupid question. Clothing. He'll need something to wear. And a dock kit. Can you put that together?" Shelton wanted to know.

"I'm pretty sure I'm capable of that. What time will he be arriving?"

"Early tomorrow." They gave me the necessary information so I could plan to go to Bethesda in the morning. It would take about four hours, so I was planning on leaving around nine. I couldn't wait to see the look on his face when I arrived.

Chapter Twenty-Four

Rusty

THE PLANE RIDE from Ramstein back to the states wasn't the greatest but I refused to complain. I was alive and that's all that counted. I don't remember anything that happened after they dragged my ass across the border. The next thing I remembered was waking up on the transport flight to Ramstein and being told I'd been shot. My first thoughts were of Lee and how she must've felt this way. Only her injuries were far worse than mine. Then I wanted to call her, but when I tried, I realized her number was in my cell phone, back in my locker at the base. I didn't count on this ... being gone this long or getting shot in the fucking leg.

As soon as they told me I was headed home, I asked the guys to meet me at the hospital with my shit. I wanted to let my girl know I was okay. Knowing her, she was worried about me. Hopefully, they wouldn't keep me long and I could get back to Drummond to show her that I was fine.

I was checked into my room and a nurse showed up to let me know my physician would be in soon to give me the rundown. They wanted to do a thorough follow up on me since that bullet had nicked my femur. The doctor at Ramstein didn't think it would pose a problem but the one here wanted to see all my tests just to be sure.

The impact to my chest knocked me to the ground. It drove all the air from my lungs and it felt like a fist had been shoved straight through my sternum. It was impossible to draw in the tiniest of breaths, and everything went gray, then turned black. Afterward, I discovered my chest was badly bruised from taking the direct shot. Kevlar was a beautiful thing, but the impact had been a fucking powerful force. I'd take the bruise any day over the actual wound. It would've killed me, no doubt.

Drifting off because I didn't sleep a whole hell of a lot on the ride over, it was her scent in my dreams that made me want her next to me. I missed that woman more than I could say. Every time I closed my eyes, I saw her strands of gold as they framed her perfect face and her Pacific Ocean eyes pulling me into their warmth. Her plump lips begged to be kissed but her smile, the one she reserved only for me, made me feel special.

The hand on my forehead had me blinking awake and the vision before me wasn't a dream at all. She was there in the flesh, smiling that perfect smile, and then bending down to kiss me.

"I never missed anyone or anything as much as I've missed you these last two weeks." My arms wound around her as we held each other tight.

"I was so worried about you when I didn't hear anything."

"My phone. Your number."

"I know." Her breath tickled my neck. "Stephen and Eric told me."

"How did they tell you?"

"I came to Virginia Beach ... to your place. I couldn't take it anymore."

"Really?" I pulled back to look at her beautiful face. "You went there to wait for me?"

"Yes. It was brutal being in Drummond and not knowing anything. I figured you'd come home first and I'd be waiting for you."

"Waiting."

"I'll always be waiting."

"You will, won't you?"

"Yes. I promise."

I only stared at her, because for two long weeks all I had was the image in my mind. Now she was real, and I was touching her. I didn't want this moment to end. "It's surreal."

"What is?"

"You being here. I can hardly believe it."

"Believe." Then she kissed me again. "You look perfect. And your beard has grown."

"Haven't shaved in two weeks. Kinda reminds me of your legs." I winked at her as she rubbed her hand over it.

"It's much more sexy than my legs, but then again, so are you."

"Stop. I haven't seen you for so long. The beast won't be able to take it."

"You're so bad." She laughed at me.

I took her hand and laid it over the beast. "See what I mean?"

Her eyes went to where her hand was and then back to

my face. "I do. Oh my. The beast doesn't seem to be affected by your injuries."

"The beast is … beastly. What can I say?"

She tried her best not to laugh by pressing her lips together. It was an epic fail.

"Tell me about what happened."

I gave her the story to best of my recollection. "My memory is foggy."

"Are you in pain?"

"Not now, but I was."

"Can I see it?"

"It's bandaged."

The door swung open and a youngish doctor came in. "Lieutenant Garrett? I'm Dr. Sanders. Can we talk?" He glanced at Lee.

"Absolutely. Anything you say to me can be said in front of her. This is Lee Marston."

"Nice to see you, Dr. Sanders." Lee held out her hand for him to shake.

"Lieutenant, I have good news. I've taken a look at all your X-Rays and tests and it appears that everything looks great as far as your femur is concerned. It should heal nicely without any long-term issues. I think in another day or two, you can be released. We need to finish these antibiotics and then set up physical therapy for you at home. How does that sound?"

"Like a great plan. Do I have any restrictions?"

"I'd like you to be non-weight bearing for another week and then use one crutch for one more. After that, let your pain predict things. How is your pain level?"

"Not bad, but then again I haven't done any walking on it."

"Let's keep it that way for the time being. I'll give you a

referral to a local physician as well, along with a pain prescription. I would like you off those ASAP."

"I haven't been taking anything for the past two days."

"Good. I'll check in on you tomorrow morning."

"Thanks, doc."

He left, and Lee said, "That's great news."

"Yeah, it is."

"I can take you home."

Lee ended up booking a hotel room for the night and two days later I was able to leave the hospital. Once we got back to my apartment, she tried to wait on me, but I forced her to let me do things for myself.

"The sooner I'm up and around, the faster I'm able to recover. Think about when you were injured. Remember how your muscles atrophied?"

"Yes. It was awful."

"That's what I'm going to avoid by doing this. I have to stay in tip-top shape for my job. If I do this, then when I'm recovered, going back will be that much easier."

"I understand."

But something was off. "Lee, what is it?"

"Nothing."

"Yes, there's something."

"Okay. Rusty, when you were gone, I was completely in the dark. I'm not sure I can do this. Living with not knowing anything … where you are … what's happening."

"Jesus, Lee. What do you want me to say? I can't tell you where we are and what our missions are all about."

She clasped her hands together and said, "I know. I realize that, but not knowing what you're doing or what's happening to you was a total mind fuck to me."

"I can imagine."

"Can you?"

I thought about it for a moment and then recognized I

couldn't. "No. You're right. Had it been you that was gone for two weeks, I would've gone crazy."

"That's what I'm talking about." Her clasped hands were now in front of her stomach, like maybe she was hurting inside. I went over to her as quickly as my stupid crutches allowed.

"I'm sorry. I really am. But what do you want me to do? I can't just quit and walk away from this. It's not how it works."

"I know. Maybe I need some distance for a while."

"You just had distance. Two week's worth. And then you told me you missed me. And you'd always be waiting. What's it gonna be, Lee?"

"I don't know. I want it without all the angst of worrying when you're gone."

I tipped her chin up and said, "I wish I could give you that. I really do. But I can't. Just like you wouldn't have been able to give it to me if you were still in the marines."

"That's unfair."

"Is it?"

She went silent on me.

"Think about it, Lee. But one thing I won't do is beg. You've known from the start what I do. And being from the military, you above anyone should've been prepared for this."

"You're right. But I guess I wasn't prepared for my heart to be so wrapped up."

Lee left the following morning. I wouldn't beg her to stay. I couldn't. As much as I cared for her, and I did, she had to figure this thing out.

"Lee, just remember, I'll be waiting for you."

She walked away, and I watched as she drove off. My heart was shattered, but there was nothing I could do.

Chapter Twenty-Five

LEE

"YOU DID WHAT?" It wasn't Mom, or even Dad who yelled the question when I walked in the door and told them why I was home. It was Glenn. "Are you crazy? What happened to my sister? The super cool girl I used to look up to?"

Mom and Dad stared open-mouthed at him.

"You don't understand, Scutt."

"Don't call me that," he snarled at me.

"Okay, then, Glenn."

"What'd he do? Treat you too good?"

"Glenn, honey, Lilou, must've had a very good reason for doing what she did," Mom said, coming to my rescue.

"Well, Lilou, what's your very good reason?" Glenn asked. My little brother who had always been my greatest ally was now one hundred percent against me.

Shame filled me, but I couldn't pretend anymore. "I

told him the truth. That I couldn't be with him not knowing where he was and worrying about him constantly while he was gone."

Glenn's glare made me fidget worse than ever. "You're forgetting something. We didn't walk away from you. We went through everything you just did when you were in Afghanistan. And we didn't leave you! What happened to you? So you gave him a verbal Dear John letter. Just like the one Great-Granddad got."

"No, I didn't do ..." But when I thought about it, that's exactly what I did. I left him because I didn't have the balls to stay. I was a coward. A spineless candy-ass. Oh fuck. I royally fucked him over. How could I have done such a thing?

"Shit!"

"Lilou, watch your language."

"Sorry, Mom, but I just ... I gotta go."

I turned around and headed back out the door. My car should have auto-pilot by now. Berating myself the entire way back to Rusty's, I prayed he'd let me in when I got there. What had I been thinking? What kind of woman was I? Yeah, it would be difficult, but what did I expect? I would have to rely on a network of friends to get me through when he was gone, but I'd do it. For him. For us.

His apartment door came into view and I barely gave my car a chance to come to a complete stop before I threw it into park. I ran—if you could call it that—to his door and banged on it with all my might. When he opened it I flew at him, almost knocking him down.

"Whoa there, girl, take it easy."

"I'm sorry. I'm an idiot. I don't know what got into me. I was a fool, a moron—" but I couldn't say another word because his mouth crashed into mine, stopping any other words from coming out.

He didn't push me away as I'd feared. He took me back without hesitation and when he stopped kissing me, he said, "I was wondering how long it would take you."

"You knew?"

"I figured once you got over the shock."

"Can we go to bed now?" I asked.

"Lee, it's the middle of the day."

"When has that ever stopped us?"

"Don't you think you should turn your car off first?"

I looked out his open door and heard my car running. Then I threw my head back and howled with laughter. "I sort of forgot." I walked outside and shut the car off.

When I got back in the door, he had a serious look on his face. "Lee, I want you to understand something. Nothing's going to change about what I do."

"I get that. It's risky and dangerous."

"And you won't ever know where I go."

"I understand that too. It's who you are. And that was you when I met you."

"I don't want this to come between us later. It's high pressure. There's no denying it. But maybe you should talk to one or two of the guy's wives. They might be able to shed some light on how they deal with it."

"Maybe. I only know once I got home Glenn gave it to me good. Told me I was just like the woman who sent my great-granddad his Dear John letter. And he was right. I'm not that person, Rusty."

"Who are you, Lee?"

"I'm the one who will always be waiting for you."

TEN MONTHS LATER

THE CAFE WAS STRUNG with tiny white lights and I never imagined it could look so … wedding-like. Jackson had placed an arbor in the corner and decorated it with a gazillion white flowers. All the tables had been pushed to the side in order to make room for seats. We hadn't invited many people, mainly family and friends. We had to keep it small enough so it could be held here. That was number one. Even though I had moved to Virginia Beach, there wasn't anywhere else I could imagine getting married.

And I'll Be Waiting … after the newspaper article appeared, the cafe took off so that now you had to have reservations a month in advance. That food channel on TV was even going to do a special on it. Jackson had hit it big. She was even opening up another restaurant here in town and Drummond was growing because people were coming here to eat and see the town.

Jackson had to enlist the help of another caterer because as my best friend, she was my maid of honor and no way was she going to be working the event. It was tough pulling her out of the kitchen that day, but I managed.

We had hair and makeup appointments that morning but then had to be back at the cafe to meet the wedding planner. The cake was arriving at noon. Wedding cake had always been my thing, so I had to be there just to make sure that went well. Afterward, we went to Mom and Dad's to get dressed.

Midnight, Rusty's sister, was also in the wedding. Rusty had asked me if she could be a part of it. As the only member of his family, and because they were so close, I wanted her in it too. Not to mention, over the last few months, she and I had gotten quite close. She met us at my parents', along with her daughter Harley, who was the flower girl. We had a party getting dressed, but Harley was the center of attention. At four years old she was adorable and the show stealer.

Once Mom and Jackson helped me with my dress, I spun around to check myself out with a critical eye. I'd chosen a plain gown of ivory crepe that was sleeveless with a jewel neckline. It had lace illusion panels at the side that actually flowed around to create the entire back of the gown. Then it had tiny satin covered buttons that ran the length of the dress. I laughed at first because Rusty was going to have a devil of a time getting me out of the damn thing.

"Well?" I asked.

Mom started to weep. "Oh, Mom, is it that bad?" I joked.

"Just hush, Lilou."

"You look stunning," Midnight said.

"Love the shoes," Jackson said.

"Me too," I giggled. They were fancy sneakers covered in satin, lace, and had sparkles all over. I had them custom made since I couldn't wear heels or any other kind of shoes on account of my prosthesis.

"Mommy, I want some of those," Harley yelled.

"I'm sure you do," Midnight said.

"All of you look gorgeous. And Harley, I'll save these shoes for you. I guess we're ready then?" I asked.

They all agreed so we went out to the waiting limo. Rusty and I decided against the first look. We wanted each of us to be surprised when I walked down the short little aisle in the cafe.

We had a small three-piece string orchestra playing for the ceremony, then we were having a DJ for the reception. Dad was waiting for me when we arrived.

The wedding planner lined us up. Rusty went down first with Harrison following as best man, and then Glenn went last. Then Midnight walked down with Harley following her. We were afraid if Jackson went before her, Harley would shoot down the aisle, chasing after her mother. When Jackson was next to the arbor, the wedding planner cued the orchestra, and Dad raised his brows. We were standing in the back and couldn't see everyone.

"You ready, pumpkin?"

"Never been more ready, Dad."

"Then let's go."

We stepped forward and that's when Rusty caught his first glance of me. Since it was summer, he was in his full dress whites, and he looked hot and sexy as hell. But he only had eyes for me and it was obvious he was pleased. He mouthed, "I love you," as I made my way toward him. My heart swelled more and more with each step I took.

At last, when Dad and I arrived, the minister asked the age-old question, "Who gives this woman in marriage?"

Dad answered, "Her mother and I." When he handed me off to Rusty, Dad said, "Take care of my baby."

"That I will, sir."

Then my hand was encased in both of Rusty's and he brought it to his lips. "You look too beautiful for any words I can express."

Stephen leaned over and said, "You're supposed to save that stuff for later."

We all chuckled.

The minister said, "I believe this couple may be in a bit of a hurry to become husband and wife."

"You bet we are. I've waited my whole life for this woman."

"I'll always be waiting for you," I said.

"Not anymore. I'm here, standing by your side, where I'll always be, in this world and the next."

The strangest thing happened then, I felt an arm go

around me, but when I looked, no one was there. Only Rusty stood next to me holding my hand. The minister spoke the vows as we said our *I dos* and he pronounced us husband and wife.

"You may kiss your bride."

"Thank you, God," Rusty said to the ceiling.

Everyone clapped as we kissed. Then I turned around and held my bouquet in the air as the music played. Rusty and I walked down the aisle and then greeted our guests, one by one.

It was great to see everyone, but hard to contain my tears when Mark, Will, and Jared, along with their wives came up to us. The spouses all cried as they greeted me and I told them I understood how much their husbands meant to them. It wasn't until I had Rusty in my life that I truly knew that. We hugged and chatted a bit while Rusty talked with the men.

Later, we made our way around the room, visiting with everyone when suddenly Rusty stopped. "Did you see him? The old man?"

"Where?" I asked.

"He just walked out the door."

"No."

"It was the old guy from the woodworking shop. Your great-granddad."

Then I knew. It was my great-granddad whose arm had been around my shoulder during the ceremony.

"He came to tell us goodbye, Rusty."

"Why?"

"Because we don't need him anymore. We found each other. Don't you see? He only helps those who need him."

Rusty nodded. "Yeah. He was waiting all this time, wasn't he?"

I leaned into him. "He was. And now he's off to wait for someone else."

THE END

If you enjoyed reading this, please consider leaving a review wherever you purchased this from. Thank you in advance.

Acknowledgements

I HOPE YOU ENJOYED READING I'LL BE WAITING, MY second contribution to The Vault. I totally loved being a part of this amazing group of talented authors, spearheaded by our leader Angel Justice. How do you know so much, Angel? It must be those wings!

Thank you to my amazing beta team—Ashley, Heather, and Kristie. You ladies are my gold. Without you, I would be a lost soul, and that's the honest truth.

No book would be complete without the input of my bestie and sometimes writing companion, Terri E. Laine. We've been through thick and thin, vanilla and chocolate, and creme brûlée and gelato together. I can't wait for our next journey to begin.

There is another person who I wouldn't know what I'd do without and that's Nasha Lama. You are the heartbeat to all my teasers, you keep my website functioning, and if it weren't for you, my newsletters wouldn't be in existence either. You are my right hand and I love you to the moon and back.

Thank you, Ellie McLove, for your awesome editing skills.

Dana Leah you totally nailed this cover. Thank you—it's perfect.

Thank you to all the Hellions in Hargrove's Hangout. I'm glad you appreciate the pictures I post.

Thank you to all of you who happen to put up with my nonsense. I mean this from the bottom of my heart. No really. I do.

And finally—thank you to all the readers who continue to buy my books. You are the reason I'm living my dream.

Included in the back is a peek of Craving Midnight, from which I'll Be Waiting is a spin-off. I hope you like it.

About A.M. Hargrove

ONE DAY, ON HER WAY HOME FROM WORK AS A SALES manager, USA Today bestselling author, A. M. Hargrove, realized her life was on fast forward and if she didn't do something soon, it would be too late to write that work of fiction she had been dreaming of her whole life. So she made a quick decision to quit her job and reinvented herself as a Naughty and Nice Romance Author.

Annie fancies herself all of the following: Reader, Writer, Dark Chocolate Lover, Ice Cream Worshipper, Coffee Drinker (swears the coffee, chocolate, and ice cream should be added as part of the USDA food groups), Lover of Grey Goose (and an extra dirty martini), #WalterTheP-uppy Lover, and if you're ever around her for more than five minutes, you'll find out she's a non-stop talker. Other than loving writing about romance, she loves hanging out with her family and binge watching TV with her husband. You can find out more about her books www.amhargrove.com.

Stalk Annie

If you would like to hear more about what's going on in my world, please subscribe to my mailing list on my website at amhargrove.com.
You can also join my private group—Hargrove's Hangout — on Facebook if you're up to some crazy shenanigans! Please stalk me. I'll love you forever if you do. Seriously.

www.amhargrove.com
Twitter @amhargrove1
www.facebook.com/amhargroveauthor
www.facebook.com/anne.m.hargrove
www.goodreads.com/amhargrove1
Instagram: amhargroveauthor
Pinterest: amhargrove1
annie@amhargrove.com

For Other Books by A.M. Hargrove visit
www.amhargrove.com

For The Love of English
For The Love of My Sexy Geek (The Vault)
A Special Obsession
Chasing Vivi
Craving Midnight
I'll Be Waiting (The Vault)
From Ashes to Flames (May 2018)
From Ice to Flames (July 2018)
From Smoke to Flames (October 2018)

Cruel and Beautiful
A Mess of a Man
One Wrong Choice
A Beautiful Sin

The Wilde Players Dirty Romance Series:
Sidelined
Fastball
Hooked

Worth Every Risk

The Edge Series:
Edge of Disaster
Shattered Edge
Kissing Fire

The Tragic Duet:
Tragically Flawed, Tragic 1
Tragic Desires, Tragic 2

The Hart Brothers Series:
Freeing Her, Book 1

A. M. HARGROVE

Freeing Him, Book 2
Kestrel, Book 3
The Fall and Rise of Kade Hart

Sabin, A Seven Novel
The Guardians of Vesturon Series

Made in United States
Orlando, FL
10 May 2022